Parker

stephanie macneil

iUniverse, Inc.
Bloomington

Parker

iUniverse books may be ordered through booksellers or by contacting:

iUniverse
1663 Liberty Drive
Bloomington, IN 47403
www.iuniverse.com
1-800-Authors (1-800-288-4677)

ISBN: 978-1-4759-6038-9 (sc)
ISBN: 978-1-4759-6039-6 (hc)
ISBN: 978-1-4759-6040-2 (e)

Library of Congress Control Number: 2012921003

Printed in the United States of America

iUniverse rev. date: 11/16/2012

For Daniel, Ms. Gloria Hay, and that kid

Acknowledgements

Thank you to Daniel Hofstede for being my first reader and providing the opinion I trust the most. For always reading every revised version of the same sentence and never complaining. For your continued support and love when I needed it most, and for believing in me. And also for the perfect choosing of Liam's name.

Thank you to Rob Bruce for reading the very first version, editing all my mistakes, and giving me your honest opinion.

Thank you to my family and friends for your support and encouragement throughout this process.

Thank you to Ms. Gloria Hay, my second-grade teacher, for writing a note in the back of a story I wrote and read to the class. I think it subconsciously stayed with me until I was inspired enough to use it.

Thank you to everyone at iUniverse. For without self-publishing I would still be out looking for someone to take a risk with me.

Most importantly, this story is for those who are going through hard times and feel that they have no one who will understand or support them. It's for those who feel alone, different, or judged for being who they are. It's for those who feel they don't have the support of their family, friends, church, school, or society. It's for anyone who is in a similar situation or is thinking about suicide—please open up and talk to someone whom you trust. You are never alone. Some great resources are the following:

Kids Help Phone (1-800-668-6868)

The Trevor Project 866-4-U-TREVOR (866-488-7386)

www.thetrevorproject.org

It Gets Better Project www.itgetsbetter.org

One

My parents thought I was suicidal, so they sent me to see a psychologist. Okay, so I guess they *knew* I was suicidal. When you end up in the hospital after slitting your wrists, it isn't questioned whether you're suicidal or not. It's obvious. Along with the social worker and the events that followed, it led me to talk about more feelings than I initially thought I had. It also helped me to figure out some stuff.

I think I've always had some degree of abandonment issues, but I guess that's just implied when you're an orphan. Or at least, I used to be an orphan. Maybe that's where everything stems from. My biological parents dropped me off at St. Catherine's Orphanage when I was born. I was told they couldn't afford to keep me. *All you need is love, right?* That place was my home for a really long time, until my new— and, as far as I'm concerned, real—parents found me, and I learned what real love truly feels like.

For as long as I can remember, whenever I felt alone or bored or angry or anything, really, I would hide away from everyone else and draw. It was my escape. So most of my time was spent in my bedroom, drawing in my sketchbook and listening to music. And thinking about him.

This is the aftermath that is my life, with all the conversations I had along the way still living inside my head.

On the corkboard above my dresser there's a photo of my best friend and me. It was taken at a sleepover last year, and he has this huge, genuine smile on his face, because my dad (behind the camera) is making him laugh. I'm smiling back at him, but there's a distant look in my eyes that isn't in his. He's never questioned me on this.

Around the photo are snapped wristbands from the neighbourhood pool and art galleries, a ticket stub from the first concert we ever went to downtown by ourselves (he has the other one), and a handful of leaves we found in the park one day last summer. They've dried up now, but he likes seeing them when he comes over, because it reminds him that summer is coming again. So I keep them up.

The sky this evening is a dark blue streaked with a luminous pink. The clouds seem to be retiring, and they create a purple hue as they become sparser and sparser. I try to recreate the image on canvas, with my watercolours bleeding into one another while the light is still available. This one will hang in Mom's office at work.

There wasn't a drop of rain in the city today, which is too bad, because I love when it rains. Every time one of us sees that it's about to start spitting, he calls the other and we go biking just to get caught in the showers. It's become an unwritten tradition.

While I'm painting, the birds perched at the top of my window, aware that I'm finished with them, take off and soar across the street to the neighbour's rooftop. This window is great for people-watching or, as Liam calls it, spying. We've been guilty on many occasions.

From downstairs, Mom yells that dinner is ready. "I'll be right down!" I yell back.

On my bed, my notebook is flipped open to a previous drawing. I'd gotten sidetracked by the sky and traded in my pencil for a paintbrush. I grab it quickly and hide it out of sight in my desk drawer.

Beautiful, symphonic Brit prog-rock fills my room before I

turn it off, grab a hoodie from the hook on my door, and run downstairs.

"What are you working on up there?" Mom asks as I slide in at the table.

"A new painting," I tell her. "The sky was too interesting not to copy. Do you want it?"

"I'll make room in my office," she says with a smile.

"How was school today, Park?" Dad asks me, steering me away from a topic I love to a topic I hate. "How did the science exam go?"

"It was okay," I say with a shrug. "I studied all night and really tried, but I'm pretty sure I just failed again. I'd just rather be drawing or something."

"You're gonna be a great artist someday," he says. "But don't forget about school just yet." He pauses for effect and then hands me a flyer he was keeping in plain view on the table. He does this act as if he'd completely forgotten that he'd staged it there for this exact purpose. I saw the paper on my way in. "By the way," he says nonchalantly. "I found this lying on the sidewalk when I was walking home from work."

Stealth, Dad.

My dad is really into being environmentally friendly, so he takes the bus or rides his bike to work every day, and he sees interesting things all the time. Taking the piece of paper from him and reading it over, I see it's for the art contest at school.

"I thought you might want to enter. It's in two weeks, which doesn't give you a lot of time, but I know you're working on something in your art class right now, aren't you?" he asks.

I break my gaze away from the flyer and look over at him. "Yeah, I am. Thanks, Dad."

We smile at each other, and then he looks over at Mom. "What happened today with the Hendersons?" he asks her.

The paper stares at me from the table. I've known about the contest for a while, but I wasn't sure whether I should enter. I've been working on my charcoal drawing at school for months now, so I guess I might as well.

They talk to themselves about work as I stare at them, with my elbow on the table and my head in my hand. My adopted parents, Mark and Sarah Knight, couldn't have kids of their own. After years of unsuccessful fertility treatments and the final realisation, they found me. It was just six weeks before I turned twelve. I don't know exactly why they chose me. I've never really asked. I've just been grateful that they did. Pretty much from the very beginning I've called them Mom and Dad, because that's just what they are to me.

Interrupting my thoughts, Dad asks, "Don't you think so?"

I look at him with a face that says *I obviously have no idea what you're talking about*. "Oh ... yeah," I say.

He smiles at me with his approving face. Apparently, I agreed with him. They go back to talking among themselves.

I'll always think of them as my real parents.

Dad cuts into my thoughts again. "We were thinking," he says, "that you could invite Liam to Kelowna for spring break."

"Seriously!" I ask, already thinking about the fun things we could do on my grandparents' vineyard in the country.

"Yeah, we thought it would be fun for you to bring someone," Mom says.

"Thanks! I'll ask him tomorrow," I say, excessively excited.

I love visiting my grandparents in Kelowna, but whenever I go, I always end up kinda bored because there's no one my age to hang out with. I have a few cousins, but sometimes they're not there. They're also all girls, so when they are there, we always disagree on what to do. They think it's fun that I have longer hair than the boys they know, but getting a makeover and having my hair in curlers is not exactly my idea of vacation. Spring break is next week, and most people already have plans, so I hope Liam doesn't. He hasn't talked about any plans, at least.

In the kitchen after dinner, Mom walks in as I'm drying my hands by the sink. She stops suddenly and looks at my wrists. I slowly look down at my shoes as I pull down my hoodie sleeves, hiding them so she can't look at them anymore. When I look back up at her, she's giving me this look she always does when she's terribly sad or worried, and tears are piled high in her eyes. I toss the dishtowel on the counter and touch her hand.

My mom is a real estate agent, and she's also the kindest person I know. When I first came to live here she hardly worked, because she wanted to be here whenever I was home, to take care of me and to get to know me. But as I've gotten older, I've had to tell her that it's okay that she works. She never lets me forget that she loves me.

"Its okay, Mom," I reassure her. "I know they'll always be there, but they're just scars now."

She takes in a deep breath and pulls me towards her in a tight hug. I smile while being smothered in her embrace. "I love you," she says.

"I love you, too."

When she releases me, she takes one last look and then lets me go. I run up to my room to get started on my really late homework.

After a shower, I stare at myself in the mirror. I have skinny arms and my ribs stick out under translucent skin. My brown hair is slightly wavy and falls a little past my jawline. I run my hands through it as I stare at my face and green eyes. Everything about me looks like a normal sixteen-year-old, until you get down to my arms. I turn my gaze to them in the mirror. Scars cross my wrists on both arms, *as if one just wasn't enough*. When I look at myself, it feels as if they take over my whole appearance. They're the only thing I see when I'm not wearing hoodies. I stare at my face again.

————————

I sat slumped in a black chair in front of my social worker, who sat with her right leg crossed over her left in another black chair across from me. We were in a white room with a window and stuffed animals piled up in a toy box. She had her dark hair pulled back into a ponytail that day. She asked questions and wrote in a book.

"And how is school going, Parker?" she asked.

Outside the window there was no questioning. I wanted to be out there.

"Uh ... school's fine," I answered.

I looked up at her then, and she was already looking at me. Her name is Clara Hampton, and she works for the adoption agency, checking in with my parents and me every now and then. The questions are pretty standard every time. She just makes sure my parents are not abusing me and that I feel safe and loved. Basic stuff like that. These "social visits" usually last about half an hour, and then I'm free from interrogation.

"It's fine," I added.

"Good, and how's home?" She wrote secrets down in her notebook. "Is there anything you'd like to talk about?"

"Uh ... no, not really. Home's good." It was the truth, for the most part.

"Good. Would you like to talk about the cuts on your wrists now?" She said it calmly and bluntly as she stared me down.

I looked at my winter-pale arms resting in my lap. Once again, I'd made the mistake of rolling up my sleeves. I tend to do that a lot. However, it was a bigger mistake back then when nobody knew about what I'd done. I pulled them down and looked at the well-worn beige carpet as I tried to think of something to say. Any lie would do. "Oh, uh ... I scratched them on the rake in the garage," I lied. "It was hanging on the wall and I wasn't paying attention walking up the steps."

Wow. There couldn't possibly have been a worse lie than that.

"Both of them?" she asked, unconvinced by my obvious lie. I shuffled in my chair to avoid the eye contact that was being forced on me. Clearly, and I don't blame her after that disaster choice of words, she didn't believe me. "What are they really from, Parker?" She didn't give up. "This is a safe place. You can tell me whatever is on your mind."

I shuffled in my chair some more. How could I possibly have told her what was on my mind? I found a strand of hair to play with, took a deep breath, and held it for a minute. The room felt hot. I could jump out that window, if it were open, I thought.

I eyed her suspiciously. At that moment, I knew she knew what I had done, so what was the harm in saying it out loud? "How do I know you won't say anything?" I asked her.

"Anything you say is confidential. It's strictly between us."

"Even my parents?" I asked.

I felt her hesitate for a moment before saying, "If I thought that something was really wrong, we would talk about it first. And if I thought it was necessary, we would then talk about it with your parents here."

Hm. Do I let it get that far? I thought. *My parents finding out?* I took another deep breath and finally decided. "I did it," I said. Even though I knew I was going to, I was still surprised to hear myself admit it. "I cut them." I finished by immediately looking down at my beat-up Chucks and waited for the lecture on the value of life and all that.

"Why did you cut them?" she then asked, so patiently.

I looked up at her. Is this how the speech about cutting yourself starts? She was still staring at me, her left leg now crossed over the right, her head tilted slightly, and her notebook and pen ready to take down everything I had to say. "I guess ... I guess I just get sad sometimes. No, *sad* isn't the word. I get depressed. I want to die sometimes." I was suddenly spilling everything, and I couldn't stop.

She continued to take everything very calmly. "What makes you sad, Parker?" she asked.

I opened my mouth to speak.

There's a knock on the door and mom's voice interrupts my memories. I'm still standing in the bathroom, still staring at myself. "Are you ready for bed, Park?" she asks from the hall.

I look at myself for a moment longer and then walk out. She's waiting for me by the banister.

"Good night, darling," she says, hugging me.

"'Night, Mom," I say. I kiss her on the cheek and go to my room.

Two

I really hate going to school. Mornings are always hectic. I wake up late and rush around the house trying to get myself ready and get all my stuff together, while Mom tries to force me to eat even though I don't have time. And the thought of actually being there makes my stomach turn. I don't do very well in school because I'm either drawing or daydreaming out the window. Or I'm trying to avoid Dylan.

A little insight: there are butterflies that occupy my stomach. I didn't ask for them to live there. And I certainly don't ask for them to fly around and cause a scene every time I see this one boy—the only boy—or every time our hands accidentally touch or every time I smell the fabric softener on his clothes. But that's how it's been for a long time. I've gotten kinda used to the butterflies, but sometimes they still take me by surprise.

They must have sensed him earlier than usual this morning, because they start to fly before I even see him walk out of his house and run down the sidewalk to me.

"Parker! I got it!" Liam yells to me as I run over to meet him halfway down the block. "My mom took me to get it yesterday. I was listening to it all night!" His big blue eyes look even more perfect today.

Oh, yeah. Those butterflies are airborne.

I take the CD as he passes it to me, look at the art on the

front cover, and flip it over to read the song list on the back. "Is it good?" I ask.

"Dude, everything he creates is genius."

Obviously. How silly of me.

"I can't wait to hear it. Hopefully my mom will drive me to the mall tonight."

"You can borrow it 'til you get yours," he offers.

"Thanks, man." I look it over once more before swinging my backpack off my shoulder and putting it in. I then look ahead and see we're getting closer to hell. "How's your mom doing?" I ask.

He shrugs. "She's not good. I mean, she pretends like she is, but I can tell. She's never really been the same since. It's just sorta obvious. But I let her think I can't tell."

He kicks a rock, and we both watch it fly and bump down the sidewalk.

My mom and Liam's mom are best friends. They became friends after I started going to school with him. When they talk on the phone, my mom sounds like a teenager, talking superfast and laughing so hard she cries. Every second Saturday, his mom and my mom go out for drinks. Dad and I can tell it was a good night when she stumbles in the front door and tries to sneak around the house as if we're sleeping. But we're always in the living room waiting to hear her stories. Over the past year, though, their conversations on the phone have been quieter, and when she comes home, she's never as eager to talk about the night out.

"My dad's getting remarried. This summer," Liam says miserably beside me. This would be news to me, but I'd overheard Mom talking to Dad about it a few days ago. Liam kicks the rock again, and we watch it collide with the concrete. "He told us two weeks ago," he says before looking at me quickly. "I would have told you sooner, but I've been hoping that it would go away. And, well, when it didn't, I just tried to forget about it."

Liam's dad starting dating this woman a couple of months

ago. Liam doesn't like her, though, because he thinks she's only interested in his dad's money and probably won't stick around for very long.

"I'm sorry, Liam. But don't worry about it. It'll be okay," I say in my most positive voice.

He gives me a weak smile.

This is my best friend, by the way: Liam Eriksson. He has long brown hair (longer and darker than mine) that falls over the left side of his face, striking blue eyes, and freckles. It's factually accurate that he's the most gorgeous boy in existence. He was the second kid to talk to me at school when I started going there four years ago, and we became instant friends. He's the kind of friend you always wish to have. And he's that kid who makes friends easily because he's so charismatic and charming, and everyone who meets him instantly loves him. We have everything in common, especially music. And especially the musicians in the band who created the CD that now rests securely in my backpack. Liam could easily be best friends with someone else, but he chose me. I'm lucky that way. He's really the only kid who's ever talked to me, except for Dylan, but it's been a long time since we were friends.

I don't really blame the other kids for not talking to me. Who would want to interfere in the life of the school bully's enemy?

"We have PE today, don't we?" He asks this beside me, but I don't hear him at first. I'm too busy thinking about the way he chews his pencils in class. "Parker?"

"Sorry, what?"

"Do we have PE today?"

"Um ... Friday—yeah, we do."

"*Great*," he says sarcastically with a roll of his eyes. I glimpse the perfect teeth in his crooked smile.

Gorgeous, I think.

"Oh," I say, remembering last night's conversation, "do you want to come to Kelowna with my family on spring break?"

"Really!" he exclaims, just as excited as I was last night at the table.

"Yeah, my parents told me to ask if you wanted to come."

"Yeah, I'll have to check with my mom first, but I'm sure she'll say yes. Tell your parents I say thanks!"

"I will."

We turn left and Liam heads onto school property and towards the steps. I stop and stand there for just a moment to watch the back of his head as he walks away, and then I run to catch up.

My locker is on the bottom and his is on top. Of course, that's just the way it goes with height. "Did you ever find your math textbook?" I ask as I'm taking a book out before first period.

"No, but it's fine," he jokes. "It was still in its wrapper, anyways."

We exchange grins, and then suddenly I feel a kick at my back, cold metal on my face, and my skin breaking as it tears down the corner of my open locker door. When it's over, I open my eyes and touch blood on my head. I turn and see Dylan walking away, laughing with his friends and staring at me as I sit on the floor.

"Queer," Dylan proclaims with disgust.

It's nothing new. I've heard them all before.

Queer. Fag. Gay.

Gay. As if I'm supposed to be offended by what I am. The same way you would call someone smart, pretty, tall, athletic, or musically gifted a name. All these things are naturally given traits, and every person has been given one. Yet, for some reason, there are people who use these features against us as a way of tearing down our self-worth. They do this because they don't feel good about themselves and don't want us to feel good about ourselves, either. *I know, it doesn't make sense.* These people are called bullies. And Dylan Baker is mine. You can't really blame these people; I mean, you can, but if you don't know their story, you don't know where the hatred grows from. Everyone faces his or her own battle. The challenge is to share these battles with each other to find common ground, and also to find people who share your fight.

Understand, though, that I'm not giving Dylan permission to use hateful words against me just because he had difficult things happen in his life when he was growing up. Everyone has. There's no free pass.

"Hey, what's wrong with you, Dylan!" Liam yells after him. He looks down at me still sitting on the floor, my protector, looking at the blood on my hand. "Parker, are you okay?" His voice is soft and caring.

"Yeah, just bleeding." I shrug it off.

"I'll take you to the nurse," he says as he helps me up.

We close our locker doors, grab our bags, and walk down the hall towards the nurse's room, while I hold my hand to my head. When we get there, Liam knocks on the door twice and then opens it, letting me in first. I walk in casually as he stays in the doorway.

"Oh dear, Parker," Nurse Maggie Hay says sympathetically in her English accent. She's not shocked to see me like this, though. "Have a seat."

I don't even wait until she says it before my bag is sitting on the floor and I'm hopping onto the bed in the room, still holding my head.

"I'll see you in class," Liam says by the door. "I'll save you a seat."

"Thanks."

He closes the door as I look at Nurse Maggie. She's eyeing me carefully, and I know what that look means. It's our unspoken secret that she knows all about my feelings for him. "Liam's a good friend," she says.

"Yeah, he is."

She takes out a handful of medical equipment and puts it all down beside me. "Let's get you fixed up," she says. She cleans away the blood on my forehead and then pours some rubbing alcohol onto a cotton ball and dabs it, while I wince through the pain.

"I suppose I should be used to the pain by now," I say. In my mind, pain has two meanings, and I know she knows this.

She puts a Band-aid over my cut. "Parker," she says, looking at me. "You should never get used to being hurt. Remember, everyone has problems. It's important to talk about them."

I jump off the bed, look at her, and then grab my bag. "Okay. Thanks, Maggie." I give her a smile before leaving.

By the lockers just outside the classroom, I carefully peer around to look through the window in the door, and I see that the room is full. I can't see Dylan, but I know he's there too, and I don't want to go in.

I turn back around and lean against the metal door, looking up at the ceiling and hoping that maybe it will feel sorry for me and come crashing down. Then we'll all have to go home. I wait, but it just stays up there. I hold my breath, swivel around on squeaky shoes, and open the door.

I slip in as quietly as I can while my teacher's back is turned to the class. I find Liam near the back of the room and sit down beside him just as Miss Fern turns around. "How nice of you to join us, Parker," she says with the smile that never ceases to find its way onto her face.

I smile slightly at her in return as she notices the Band-aid. She gives me a nod before turning back around to the board, and I start my search for Dylan.

He's sitting on the other side of the classroom by the windows, where we used to sit, and he's glaring at me. I'm grateful to Liam for finding seats on this side at the last minute. Maybe he bartered with someone else to trade.

My elbow on the desk shields Dylan from my view as I rest my head in my hand. He and I used to be friends, and he was actually the first kid to ever talk to me at this school. Dylan, Liam, and I were all good friends. But then, about two years ago, things changed.

Miss Fern writes math equations on the board, but I can't pay attention, so I let my mind wander.

————————

It was the end of summer. Only a few more days until Grade 8 would start. It was an afternoon on a scorching hot day, and I was spending it inside. I was sitting on my bed and in the middle of finishing a drawing in my sketchbook when Dylan came bursting into my room. It was so sudden. If I had known he was coming over, I would have had the book hidden by the time he got there. I quickly jumped off my bed and ran over to the desk. The drawer was open, but I just wasn't quick enough, and he snatched it out of my hands.

"What are you drawing?" he asked, looking at it and then holding it up to me to reveal the half-shaded face of a guy on the thick paper. I couldn't do anything but just stand in front of him, looking at my shoes and around the room. "Who's this, your boyfriend?" he teased.

I grabbed the book out of his hands and shoved it into the open drawer. "Just a drawing."

He just laughed at me as I looked at the floor. I'd managed to escape that, I thought. "Okay," he said finally. "Well, do you wanna go to the pool to watch the girls again?"

"Um ... no. I have to help my mom out with some stuff today," I said. That lie probably would've worked if it were colder outside, but like I said, it was the end of August, and there was no hiding the sweltering heat outside.

"I heard Amber's going to be there," he said, trying to persuade me with the girl he thought was the hottest in our class.

"I have to stay home."

"Okay, well, do you want to come tomorrow? It's going to be the hottest day of the summer."

"No, I don't think I can."

His expression dropped suddenly, and the temperature in

the room rose. He looked at me, confused and angry. "What's with you lately? You've been acting really weird."

I felt my face begin to burn red. "No, I haven't," I said defensively.

"You have. You never come to the pool or anywhere with us anymore, because you're always hiding at home, drawing. You've been in here the entire summer!"

"That's not true," I protested.

"Oh yeah, you came for one week at the very beginning of the summer. Big deal," he said. "And why do you hide everything, anyways? You never let us see what you're keeping in that stupid notebook."

"Dylan, just stop, please."

"No. Tell me what's going on."

He was staring at me so hard. I could feel it even though I was looking at the floor. A part of me knew I wouldn't be able to keep this a secret forever, but I hadn't thought it would happen like this. When I'd told my parents, they'd said that they already knew. I don't know how they knew, but they were okay with it. Kids, however, are mean. I made up my mind, prepared myself for the storm, and lifted my emotionally heavy head to face him.

"I'm gay, Dylan." The words barely escaped my trembling lips, but I had finally said it.

He laughed. "No you're not. Come on, let's go!"

Now I couldn't stop looking at him. "Dylan. I am."

His smile faded and he stared at me, confused again. "I don't get it. You like guys now?" He cringed.

"Not just now. I always have."

"So that's what the picture is about?"

I shrugged.

He looked around the room and ran his hand through his short blond hair. "Oh. Um … okay. I … I have to go now. I'll see you around, Parker." And then he was gone. I stood there in my room, thinking to myself how that couldn't possibly have been worse. I stared at the door, half expecting him to come back in and say something, but he didn't.

Nothing could have prepared me for what followed over the years. The storm that was Dylan.

––––––––––

Something hits the back of my head and it's followed by laughter from the back corner. A paper airplane falls to the tiled floor, and I notice that Miss Fern isn't at the front anymore. That's how they do it. When the teacher's gone, they do whatever they like.

The bell rings and everyone heads to the door all at once as if they're trying to exit a concert. Beside me, Liam pulls his bag over his shoulder. I haven't even thought about getting up yet. "Are you coming, Parker?" he asks.

"Yeah. In a minute."

He puts his hand on my shoulder. My heart rate begins to run faster. The butterflies that were once sleeping have now awoken. I have to force myself with all my strength not to touch him back. "Don't let them get to you. They're stupid, and they're just trying to get a reaction out of you."

I know he's right. We've watched enough inspirational TV movies over the years to not know that. "Thanks. I'll be right there."

The halls are crowded as I push through to the bathroom. I quickly check under the stalls for signs of people and then escape into the second one, locking the door. The ceiling is my focus. I'm hoping that looking up will force the tears to stay in my head instead of falling down my face. I try to fight it, but I'm not strong enough. Soon there they are. Silent tears slipping down.

The bathroom door creaks open, and someone comes in. I hear him lock a stall door a couple down from mine. I quickly wipe my face with my sleeve and walk out.

Other than a few pieces of paper littering the floor, the hallway is empty. I didn't even hear the end-of-break bell ring. I walk back in the direction I came from, knowing I'm not going back to class. Ducking under the classroom windows so no one will see me, I run as fast as I can to the exit doors and leave.

By the time I'm almost home I've run so fast and I'm so out of breath it probably looks as if I'm being chased. I stop to consider my options, as I rest my forearms on my thighs and catch my breath. If I go home, no one will be there, and I can just hide out with no one knowing. The school will call my house when they find out I'm missing, but my parents won't be there to answer it.

There is no other option. I can't go back there.

My phone vibrates in my pocket, and I dig it out to check it. It's a text from Liam, asking where I am. It's the first of two texts. I ignore it and return it to my back pocket. He'd only come after me if he knew I was skipping, and right now I just want to be alone.

The house is quiet when I walk in, but you can never be too sure, so I call out for my parents. When no one answers, I drop my bag by the stairs and head to my room. I play the CD Liam lent me before I fall onto my bed and stare at the posters on my walls.

Dylan didn't always seem so mean. Or maybe I just never noticed it until it was directed at me. He lives ten minutes away from me, and it's just him and his mom. He's never met his dad. That's one thing we have in common, but I guess you need more than one bond to be friends. His mom is nice, but she always had a different guy over, and I thought that must have been hard for Dylan. Either that or she would be out all night. I think that must be difficult for him, too. Sometimes when Liam and I would sleep over at his house, we'd have to make sure all the windows and doors were locked, and even lock Dylan's bedroom door, because she wasn't around. I never told my parents that. They would have freaked out if they knew that three twelve-year-olds were alone all night. I didn't want to get anyone in trouble. Thinking about it wears me out, so I close my eyes.

The knocking on my bedroom door later wakes me up. "Parker?" I hear Mom call from the hall. I mumble something that I think are words, and she walks in, holding my backpack. "Hey, Park. Were you sleeping?"

I nod and yawn as I sit up. *How long was I asleep?*

"Okay, well, I just wanted to give you your backpack. Not that you have any homework with you, do you?" She says this with a sly look on her face, which means she knows. I shake my head slowly while watching her cautiously. "The school called my office after they called the house and got no answer. Your dad came home early to check if you were here."

And that is as far as sneaky goes for a sixteen-year-old.

Now she looks at me with sadness. "How far did you get today?"

"The end of first period."

She smiles at me sympathetically and touches the Band-aid on my forehead. "What happened here?" she asks.

It's no use trying to think of a lie for her. Embarrassed, I stare down at the bed and run my fingers along the seams of the blanket.

"It will get better you know, Parker." She has such conviction in her voice. If I wasn't so sad, I might actually believe her. She brushes my hair with her hand and holds the side of my face while looking at me. "Sometimes," she says, "problems don't go away completely, but one day it won't feel so heavy."

I try to think about the future. About not being in high school, about not having to see Dylan every day, about not getting my head bashed into sharp objects. I can't, though. All I see is today. Today hurts.

Suddenly the doorbell rings. She leans over and kisses me on the forehead. She smells so good, like a vanilla meadow. She gets up to answer the door. "Thanks, Mom," I say when she's standing in the doorway. She turns to smile at me and then she's gone.

I lean against the headboard and check my phone again. Seven more texts and three calls from Liam, wondering where

I am and am I okay. A few seconds later, a neutral-faced Liam comes through the door. His low level mood takes a turn upwards as he looks around the room and just about explodes with excitement when he hears the music. "This new album is incredible!" he screams into the room, staring at nothing in particular, just lost in his mind at how good it really is.

I laugh at him. "Yeah, it's amazing."

"It's the best they've ever done!" he exclaims. I agree with him as he calms down and sits on the bed with me. "You know, the whole idea of texting is that when someone texts you, you text them back," he teases me.

"I'm sorry. I just wanted to be alone. And I just couldn't be there," I say. "I had to get away."

"Yeah, I get it."

He doesn't tell me he was worried about me. He doesn't say he was thinking about me. He doesn't convey that he needed me in any way. And I don't expect him to say or feel any of these things. I just want him to.

Instead, he simply stares at me with his familiar look of concern. But it doesn't stick around for very long before a smirk breaks out on his face. "You missed PE," he says.

I mirror his grin. "I bet it was great."

"Oh, it was," he says sarcastically. We laugh over how much we both hate gym class, and then his face turns concerned again. "So ... do you wanna talk about it?" he asks.

"I don't know. I just want to forget about it."

"Yeah, I know."

And I know he does.

We're quiet for a while, looking at our hands on the bed, until I finally break down and say, "We used to be friends; then one day he hates me. I just don't get it."

"I guess some people just can't handle the difficult stuff. You'll always have me, though, Parker."

When he says this, something in me decides on its own to move my hand an inch closer to his, but as soon as I watch it happen, I quickly retract my fingers to where they were and stare hard at my knee. I feel him watching me as my face starts to burn red. *Why did I do that?* Then without warning, I feel his hand touch mine. I look up to find his eyes suddenly locked with mine. My heart is beating fast. It won't stop thrashing against my ribcage. I feel dizzy at the sensation of his soft hand. His fingertips lightly weigh down the veins under my skin.

"Always," he says.

My bedroom door flies open suddenly, and we pull our hands away from each other. My stomach flutters when our fingers slide down to the tips, and we blush at the thought of being caught. Mom leans on the doorframe. "Your dad and I are heading out," she says. "There's a frozen pizza in the freezer. Liam, you're welcome to stay over if you'd like."

Some kids have a voice for their friends and one for friends' parents, but Liam only has one. "Thank you, Mrs. Knight," he says sweetly.

"We should be back in a couple of hours," she continues. "You boys have fun. I love you."

"Love you too, Mom."

"Goodbye, Mrs. Knight!"

She smiles at us before closing the door.

"Your mom's great. I can't stay, though. I'm supposed to be at my dad's soon." He dramatically falls back on my bed and covers his face with his hands. His shirt rides up, revealing blue cotton boxers and perfect skin between his jeans and band T. I try to look at something else, like the window—something I won't think about while trying to fall asleep tonight. "I can't believe he's marrying her!" he complains, his voice muffled by his hands.

My gaze eventually falls back to him. I watch as his chest rises and falls, and I think about his heart pumping. Then I think about how fast my own is going, and I wonder if he can hear it. "At least you don't have to live with them," I say.

"Yeah, thank goodness!" he exclaims and pulls himself back up to a sitting position. "I should get going." I direct my view to the wall, anything that isn't him, as he walks over to the door. "I'll call you tomorrow, Park," he says. "Oh, and my mom said I can go to Kelowna with you. She's going to call your mom tomorrow."

"Okay—sweet! I hope you survive tonight!" I say, half kidding, half serious, and I wave as he makes a silly face at the door and then closes it behind him.

After he leaves, I remain sitting on my bed for a while. My alarm clock reads 5:36, which means I've slept for a really long time. I look around the room, still listening to the music, and think about him running down the stairs and out of my house.

I don't know the exact moment when I fell in love with Liam. All I know is that I did, and I can't do anything about it. I really hope he doesn't know, though. He's my best friend. I can't risk losing him.

Three

My first day of Grade 7 was so nerve-wracking. I had never been to school before, and I didn't want anybody knowing that. People look at you different when they find out you're adopted. I hate that look. I just wanted to be a normal kid for once in my life. I walked into the strange classroom and looked around. There were kids everywhere, all laughing and talking to their friends. I hoped so badly that I would make just one friend. I found an empty desk in the middle of the room and sat down. After a couple seconds, two of them came over and stood in front of me.

"Hey, you're new here," one of the boys said. I guess I stood out among the rest of them. It was *my* first day, but just another one for everyone else.

"Hi … yeah, I am," I said softly.

"I'm Dylan, and this is Liam," he said pointing to the other kid. "You can sit with us if you want."

"Okay, thanks."

I was surprised and relieved by how smoothly this was going. When we sat down at three empty desks, Liam turned to me, "So what school did you go to before?" he asked. I couldn't tell him I went to school at the orphanage, so I said I was homeschooled. It was basically the truth. "I have cousins who are homeschooled," he told me. "They hate it. Did you like it?"

"It was okay, I guess."

———————

A crash in the kitchen wakes me up from my nap on the couch, and I turn around quickly to see a giant rock sitting amongst shattered glass from the patio door in the kitchen. I don't have to think hard about who did it. I quickly run to the front porch just as three kids run down the street. Dylan's friends Ethan and Avery follow him everywhere as if they're one person. There's never a time when I get hit in the face or kicked on the soccer field or yelled at in the hall that they're not right there behind him. I honestly don't know why they hang out with him. They always seemed okay and not very mean at all, in my opinion. A part of me is glad they're far away when I get there. I don't know what I'd do if they wanted to fight. My only defence is Liam and running away.

As I'm dumping the rest of the glass into the trash under the sink, I hear the front door open and my parents' laughter enter the house. I quickly throw the broom and dustpan into the pantry just as they walk in. Their eyes go from me to the door, and the laughter stops. There's no hiding the spring air entering into the room.

"Parker, what happened?" Dad asks. I can't bring myself to tell them, so I just look at the floor. He walks over to me, puts a hand on my shoulder, and kneels down a little so we can be eye to eye. "Parker," he says. "Was it who I think it was?"

My dad towers over me with his dark hair and brown eyes. A lot of people mistake us for being related because we look so much alike, although I'm obviously a lot shorter than he is. He's a contractor for an architectural firm, and he's a vegetarian, like Mom and me, with a kind and sensitive heart. He's always trying to make me try new foods, even when they don't look like food. He has the best laugh I've ever heard, and his favourite thing to do is play street hockey with me, which I'm not very good at, but he loves it.

I still can't force out any words. I look over at Mom, and she nods. Finally, I look back at him and say, "Yes."

I see the anger in his eyes as he lets go of me. I know he isn't angry with me, but I still feel bad. "Thank you, Parker. You should get to bed now."

In the bathroom, I stand in front of the mirror and stare at myself. I start the shower before taking off my hoodie and throwing it on the floor in frustration. My wrists stare at me through the mirror. I want to escape this world and forget about my life. I throw my shirt onto the pile that is forming in the corner by the door. I'm breathing hard, but I just continue to stare.

––––––––––

I sat on a brown leather sofa in a dark-panelled room on the twenty-seventh floor of an office building. It had a big window overlooking the city of Vancouver. The psychologist sat in front of me in a big brown chair, with one leg crossed over the other. I wondered if every person who worked with social situations knew to sit like that. Maybe they taught it in school, I thought. He held a pen in his hand and a notebook balanced on his knee. I watched as it tilted from side to side.

He looked a little dishevelled, which took me by surprise for a moment. I thought these people were supposed to be clean-cut and distinguished, but he looked as if he hadn't shaved in a couple days, and he looked like he had more on his mind than I did on mine. I decided that he was probably fifty. He started asking me questions and scribbling short notes in his book, when it wasn't almost falling to the floor. I liked that he had an understanding voice under all the scruff. It was the kind you would hope for in someone you were about to see for a long time.

"So tell me, Parker," he said. "Why are you here?"

I was there because I had caused so much damage in my life. I was there because I had no choice. I was there because there had been a lot of blood.

I didn't say any of those things, though. I simply looked around the room. There were hundreds of books on the shelves, and he had diplomas and certificates covering the wall over his desk, which made him look legitimate.

Then I finally looked at him. "My parents think I have suicidal thoughts," I said.

He stared through me, reaching to my soul. "And are they right?" he asked. "Do you have thoughts of suicide?"

"Yeah. I guess so," I said plainly.

"I see. And what provokes these thoughts?" I was quiet for a while, thinking about my answer and staring at the dark-coloured carpet. I traced the diamond pattern with my eyes. "Would it be correct to say that you think of committing suicide?" he asked.

"Yeah," I said honestly.

"You were taken to the emergency room, yes?"

"Yes."

"What did that feel like?"

"Scary."

And then he asked me a question I didn't expect him to ask. But I don't know why I didn't expect it. "Why? Why was it scary?"

I hadn't thought about that before. I tried to think back to the moment when I woke up. The moment I didn't anticipate to happen. "My parents," I said.

"What about them?" he asked.

"The look in their eyes. They looked so sad."

"Did you think they were going to be mad at you?"

I nodded. "Yeah. But that was what I thought I was going to avoid."

"Please explain."

"I thought that by the time they found me, I would've already been dead. I wouldn't have been able to feel how mad they were at me." And then without thinking, I added, "And then they wouldn't be able to send me back to school."

"What's at school?" he asked. He even sat up a little, as if he had uncovered something interesting and wanted to dig further into it.

I'd said too much. I didn't want to say anymore and give him a reason to make me talk about my feelings. I avoided all the eye contact he was trying to make and fixated my attention on a painting by the door. It was hard to tell exactly what it was, some sort of abstract or something. There was a whole mess of colours. They had all been painted across the canvas and ultimately mixed with one another. There was something underneath all the colours, too, but I couldn't quite make it out.

Suddenly he changed topics and began talking again. It caught me off guard, after I'd been staring at the painting so intently, and made me jump. "Why did you cut your wrists?" he asked.

"I was angry," I answered on reflex.

"Angry enough to put yourself in so much danger?" I decided not to answer and went back to looking at the diamond carpet. "Death is a huge commitment," he said.

I thought it was weird that he used the word *commitment*. As if it were a relationship we were talking about. "I wanted to get out," I told him. "I wanted to escape." Where was all this coming from? I thought. And why was I telling him? I didn't even know him. But it was like it was just gushing out, and I couldn't control or filter any of it. I looked up at him then, before looking back down at my shoes. "More than anything," I said, more quietly than before, "I just wanted the pain to stop."

"What pain do you feel, Parker? What gives you pain?"

I looked up at him again. I was here for a reason, right? I might as well say it. Plus I didn't want to be here for any longer than I had to. "Kids in my class. One kid in particular."

"What do they do?"

"They make fun of me. They push me around when there are no teachers watching."

"Why do they do this?"

I looked straight into his eyes and inhaled. "Because I'm gay." It seemed a lot scarier in my mind than when it left my mouth. His face didn't change at all.

"I see. And what do you do after they hurt you?" he asked.

"I hurt myself … I cut myself … my wrists."

"And this makes the pain go away?"

"No. But for a minute, when I'm doing it, I don't think about the pain they put me through. I only think about the pain in my arms."

"And the last time you did this was supposed to be your suicide?" he asked calmly. *How morbid to talk about my suicide*, I thought. But I nodded nonetheless. "Why was that time so final?"

Final.

Again with the words.

"I'd had enough," I told him. "I'd decided I couldn't take it anymore."

He nodded, which I thought was odd. I thought that after I hadn't gotten one from Clara, I'd for sure I'd get a lecture from him on all the wonderful things in life I'd miss out on. Instead, he asked, "Do you have anyone your age you talk to about this?"

I looked at the books on the shelves again and tried to read the titles, while I wondered if he was trying to get rid of me. Then I turned back to him. "My best friend, Liam. I talk to him."

"And Liam listens to you?"

"Yeah."

"And he understands you?"

"Sometimes I think he's the only person in the whole world who really understands me."

———————

When I finally fade back to reality, I'm standing under hot water in the shower. I let the water just run over me as I think about that moment two years ago. Then the tears come, and I can't help but cry for a long time. I really thought killing myself would just make everything better. It made perfect sense. If I were dead, I wouldn't have to get kicked around by Dylan and his friends anymore. I wouldn't have to make so many trips to the nurse's room and wouldn't have to bring so many bandages home. I wouldn't have to stand in front of my mother while she looked at me as if I were her favourite vase smashed into pieces on the floor.

I would be free.

When you live every day afraid of the next, anything seems better, even bleeding on your bedroom floor. But that's no way for anyone to live, being afraid.

Looking back, I realize how lucky I was. I had incredible parents who gave me a home, loved me, and would do anything for me, even though I'm not related to them. They accepted and even embraced the fact that I'm gay and never treated me any differently. And I had a best friend who always looked out for me and had my back every time I fell. He listened every time I bawled my eyes out on his shoulder and told me times wouldn't always be this tough. But sometimes that doesn't matter at the time.

It's like a blur in your peripheral vision when all you can see is the terror in front of you. And the future is too far off to even think that easy times could be out there. I didn't think about anyone but myself, because at the time no one else mattered.

I hated the fact that I was being forced to bleed in the hallway because I'm gay. I thought that it must have been my fault somehow and I must have brought it on myself. When you're not what society portrays as a first-class citizen, you feel wrong, and sometimes it's really hard to deal with.

I know now that it isn't a fault. It's who I am, and there's nothing wrong with that. There's an endless number of differences in the world. I see now how Liam and my parents helped me by never making me feel that I was wrong, and I'll always be grateful to them for that.

I stopped cutting myself after I had seen the psychologist

for six weeks. I think I grew quite a bit in that short period of time. It was as if something clicked inside my head and told me that my parents wouldn't have sent me there if they didn't care about me and want me to get better. Most importantly though, *I* wanted to get better. So I decided that I wanted to live. If the only reason why I was dying was because a kid at school didn't like what I was, then I had to get a different reason. The thing about that, though, was that there wasn't a different reason—no different one and no better one.

Who cared if he didn't like me? I was beginning to like me. I was starting to be okay with the life I had. Because being gay didn't mean the end of the world. Maybe it was a more difficult one, but it was one I wanted to explore. A voice in my head told me there were things made just for me and they were waiting for me. I couldn't discover them if I was dead. Yes, it would be a struggle, but I now wanted to see if it was worth it. I wanted to learn and grow, to discover what I was good at and what I'd been born to do, and to love and be loved. *Really* love and be loved. By someone who's been down the same road as me. Because those *are* things to live for—for everyone. I just needed to hold on a little longer. I'm glad now that I decided to live. Maybe the boy I'm supposed to be with isn't Liam, but I know that, no matter what, I'll always have Liam as my best friend, and that in itself is a reason to stay alive.

There has to always be hope. Hope will help us see a better day.

It's still hard to go to school and live my life, but having people to talk to helps. Even when you think there's no one to listen to you, there is.

———

In bed tonight, I can't get Liam out of my head. Three years ago, the three of us spent every day together until partway into the summer. This was before they found out and Dylan turned my life into hell.

We were at our neighbourhood pool the first week school let out after Grade 7. It was the fifth time that week we had been there, and Dylan couldn't wait to get outside. He was jumping impatiently by the door of the locker room. "You guys are too slow! I'll meet you out there!" he told us, already halfway out the door.

"Okay, Dylan," I said.

It was just Liam and me. I opened the locker door, pulled off my shirt, and threw it inside. From the edge of the locker, I watched Liam take off his shirt. I lingered for a moment before he turned around, careful not to get caught. He threw it into the locker with mine and smiled at me. I smiled back.

That day at the pool was one of the last times I went there that summer. Surrounded by so many people, I was afraid someone would make an offhand comment and I'd be stuck in the middle of it. I wasn't about to let that happen.

My bedroom door opens slowly and I watch as Mom steps in and sits down beside me on my bed. She puts her hand on mine. "You had a rough day today, huh?" she asks after a second. I can only nod, overwhelmed by so many emotions stuffed up in my head and trying hard to choke back tears. "I'm so sorry you had to go through that, darling."

I break down and start to cry, trying to take in air through sobs as she wipes away the tears. "It's not fair, Mom. They did it because I don't like girls. Because I'm not like them."

She brushes her fingers through my hair while looking at me endearingly. "I'm glad you're not like them," she says. "Those other boys are mean, but you have the kindest heart I have ever had the privilege of knowing."

Even though I know now that being different is okay, I guess I still just need to be reminded of it every now and then.

"Do you hate that I'm different, Mom?" I ask her. "Do you ever wish I wasn't? What happens when I bring a boy over? Don't you think it would just be easier the other way?"

She smiles at all my questions and then thinks about something for a minute while continuing to comb her fingers through my hair. "When I found out that I would never be able to have children," she says, "I was incredibly sad and angry, for a very long time. But one day I woke up and realized that my pain was nothing compared to that of a child without any parents." She stops to take my hand in hers and then continues, "When we first saw you, Parker, we fell in love. We knew right away that you were always supposed to be ours. We didn't know from that instant that you were gay, but even if we had we still would have taken you home, because you're ours. And because it doesn't matter. It's as simple as that. We love everything about you, and we would never change a single thing. I still wake up every morning grateful that you're ours." She pauses again and squeezes my hand to make sure I'm still paying attention to this important part. "Everyone's different, Parker," she says. "And in that sense, you are no different than anyone else. Differences are special and unique, and you should embrace your difference instead of hiding it away. Don't ever think you're alone. You're not the only one who's gay."

I stare up at her and laugh a little, while tears fall down my face. She wipes them away and then kisses my forehead. What a silly thing it is to think that. Of course I'm not the only one who's gay. There are other people like me. Maybe not at school, but they're out there. I'll find them some day. The way she says it, though, makes me laugh, and I feel a little bit better.

"And don't worry about bringing a boy home," she says. "As long as he loves hockey, he and Dad will get along just fine."

"And you?" I ask.

"As long as he loves you," she says as she opens the door. "Get some sleep now, baby."

"I love you, Mom. And Dad too."

"We love you too, hun."

She leaves my room, and I hear Dad's voice outside in the hall immediately. "I can't believe what those kids are doing to him," he says before the door is closed completely.

"Shh, Mark; he'll hear you," Mom says.

"It's not right, Sarah! He shouldn't have to deal with this. I'm going to talk to his principal Monday morning."

"I know he shouldn't have to. It's not fair. But doing that will only make things worse for him. Come on, let's go to bed."

I wait until I hear their bedroom door close before I start crying again. I pray that my dad won't talk to my principal.

Four

My hand drags across the neighbour's white picket fence as I walk to school. I see Mr. Rube planting flowers in his garden. He looks up, and we wave to each other as I wait for Liam to come out of his house. Yesterday I begged my dad for hours not to talk to my principal. He reluctantly said he wouldn't, and I'm grateful. I really don't need to give Dylan another reason to hate me by telling on him.

At school I can't concentrate. I take notes, but I don't know what I'm writing. Beside me, I can hear Liam scribbling down words on his paper. Every day it gets harder and harder to resist my hand touching his. I peer through the corner of my eye at him for a just a second and then look away.

This week the school guidance counsellor is meeting with all the students about our futures and applying to colleges. You know, really fun stuff. Everyone with last names A–F went this morning. During the afternoon, it's G–L.

I step into Mrs. Sharpe's office and sit in the empty red chair in front of her desk. A stack of binders and papers currently occupies the other chair. She looks happy to see me. "So, Parker," she says with a great big smile. Her glasses slip down her thin nose, and she adjusts them. "How's school going?"

I shrug. I know she expects me to say something more, but I just shrug. I feel as if there's a weight hovering over us. She doesn't press the issue, though. Instead, she takes out a folder with my name and picture on it. It's a terrible picture. I woke up late on picture day and threw on whatever was closest to the door. Mom hates it that I didn't brush my hair.

"Your grades are average, but you still have time to improve them before college applications are sent away."

"Why do we have to start thinking about college now?" I ask. "I'm only in Grade 10."

"Better to start now than to put it off until it's too late. Schools like to at least see that you're interested, even though your Grade 10 marks won't matter much."

Can't argue with logic.

"What kind of schools are you interested in?" she asks.

"I haven't really thought about it."

"What interests you?" I take a moment to ponder, but she doesn't wait for me. "You're doing very well in art," she says proudly after flipping through my marks from last semester. I nod. "Not so good in PE," she says, almost frowning at another page. As if I'm hoping for a football scholarship. I nod again. "Maybe an art school would interest you?"

"I honestly haven't even thought about it."

She rolls over to a filing cabinet, shuffles through papers inside, and then rolls back. She arranges pamphlets like a fan on the desk. "These are all great schools for the arts." I survey them with a careful *hmm* because I think that's what she wants me to do. "Do you think you'll want to stay in the city?"

I haven't thought about that, either. The farthest I've ever been is Kelowna. Suddenly I think about Liam. What if he's planning to leave the city? Or the province? The country? What if he goes far away to study music? Like Europe. He's always talking about how all the best metal bands come from Europe. I try not to think about him leaving me. But I feel as if I'm suffocating.

"I don't know," I manage to cough up.

She seems unconcerned about my inability to breathe and starts listing off all my choices. Stuff like graphic art and designing for videogames. Other things like makeup artistry and costume design. "Any of these sound interesting to you?" she finally asks.

"I have no idea," I say honestly.

She looks at me like I've failed life.

"Well," she says after a moment, "Take these with you. Look them over with your parents, and we can arrange another time to talk over your options."

I thank her and leave. I wish I knew exactly what I wanted. It would make this life thing a whole lot easier.

Mrs. Sharpe is right about one thing. I'm not good at gym. Not in the slightest. I hate it as much as it hates me. When you're a kid with no athletic ability, it's just another reason to be made fun of. I'm just the skinny kid with long hair who likes art, and I don't belong there.

On our way back to the locker rooms after an intense hour of trying to dodge all the balls played in that wretched game, I get the air knocked out of me and fall onto my butt by yet another yellow plastic dodgeball thrown by Dylan.

"Dylan!" Mr. Van Dorsen's voice echoes throughout the gym as he reprimands him.

Dylan and his friends walk past and laugh to themselves. "Loser," he says to me as I stare up at him from the floor.

I sit there for a minute watching them walk away. Then Liam holds out his hand, and I have to resist the urge to pull him down with me. To feel his weight on me.

"Are you okay?" he asks, his blue eyes full of concern for me.

Instead, I let him help me up. "Yeah, I'm fine."

We both stand in the empty gym and watch the entrance to the locker room, neither of us wanting to go in there.

Third period is art class. It's the only thing I actually like about school. It's finally something I'm good at. I think anyone can be good at art if they try, because art is personal. You just create what you feel, and no one can tell you it's wrong. Liam isn't in my class, because he takes music third period,

"Yes. And over the years, we've seemed to have tried everything: talking to them, trying to solve the problem. Then, when that didn't work, separating them on different sides of the room—"

"Putting them in different classes," Mr. Morrison finishes his sentence.

This is a game to them.

"But nothing's seemed to work, and I'm afraid that if we don't do anything to stop it, it'll simply escalate. And I can't jeopardize my son's safety," Dad says.

"Well, as you know, I've called in Mrs. Baker to come talk today, too. I thought the five of us together would be able to come up with some sort of arrangement."

"I certainly hope so. I can't even count the number of times Parker's come home crying from school."

"Dad!" I can't believe he just told him that.

"Do you want help or not?" he asks me sternly.

"No! I never asked for help! You said yesterday that you weren't going to do this, and I was glad. I don't want it!"

"Well, I'm sorry, but this is the only way I know how to help you anymore."

The receptionist buzzes in on the phone and tells us that Dylan's mom is here.

I can't take it.

I can't do it.

I can't breathe in here.

It's so hot.

He's about to send them in.

I can't breathe.

"Please. Please don't send them in," I beg while starting to breathe faster and dramatically clasping my hand to my chest.

Mr. Morrison looks at me, concerned, and then looks at Dad. "Is he okay?" he asks.

Dad stares at me too. "Parker?"

I hear their voices fade as the room spins.

When I wake up, I'm in the nurse's room, lying on the bed. Nurse Maggie is hovering over me holding a bag of ice to my head.

"Good afternoon," she says. I don't say anything. I'm trying to figure out where I am. "You passed out in the principal's office. Do you remember that?"

I shake my head.

"Do you remember being there at all?"

I nod my head.

She looks relieved. "Good, we won't have to send you to the hospital after all." I stare at her as she moves the cold bag around on my head. "I've been telling them they need to get better circulation in this place. Maybe you're just the thing to convince them!" she says optimistically.

I sit up a little and notice that my head is killing me. "Where's my dad?" I ask.

"He's outside, sweetie, and he's worried sick."

"What about—"

"She's gone home, don't you worry. And Dylan's back in class. A place you won't be going back to today."

"Is he mad?"

"Who? Dylan or your dad?"

"I don't know."

"Well, Dylan, yes, because he's always mad at something. But you're dad isn't mad. He's just worried, that's all."

"I hate this."

"I know, dear."

"It's all my fault."

"What do you mean?"

"I should be able to stick up for myself around Dylan. Or I should've at least gotten better at it by now. My parents shouldn't have to come down here and fight my battles for me."

"It's noble of you to want to do this without help, but sometimes in life you have to ask for it. And there's nothing wrong with that. A parent's job is to protect their child from the dangers of the world. Your danger just so happens to be an angry sixteen-year-old boy. Don't feel bad about anything. Just be glad that you have a dad who is willing to stand up for you, no matter what."

I try to smile, but my head hurts too much to make the muscles in my mouth move. "How long have I been here?"

"Just a few minutes. Are you ready to go?"

I nod.

Outside, Dad is waiting in a chair against the wall. He gets up quickly when the door opens. "Hey, Park. How do you feel?" he asks.

"I'm okay. My head hurts."

"Well, let's just get you home. Thank you, Mrs. Hay," he says to Nurse Maggie.

"Feel better, Parker," she says.

Halfway down the hall, Dad says, "Mr. Morrison came by a little while ago and said he wasn't sure if having another meeting with you kids there would be a good idea, so we decided to meet with just the parents sometime after spring break. How does that sound?"

The stuff that Nurse Maggie had said about letting them help me swam around in my head for a second, and I figured I really had no choice. "Okay."

"Do you want to get some ice cream?" he asks. I nod my head, and he wraps his arm around me. Normally, I would've tried to get free if there was anyone watching, but the hall is empty, so I let him.

"Parker!" I hear from down the hall. I guess it isn't *that* empty. Liam is running towards us when I turn around.

"I'll meet you in the car," Dad says before leaving.

"Hey," I say when Liam gets to me.

"Hey. What happened to your head?"

"Oh ... I passed out."

"Doing what?"

"Panicking."

"Oh." A faint smile creeps onto his face and then onto

mine, as I realize how silly it is that I fainted from thinking too hard. "Are you okay now?"

"Yeah, but I'm going home."

"Okay. Do you want to hang out later?"

"Sure, if my head ever stops hurting."

"How about tomorrow?"

"Okay." I feel the butterflies start to fly around as I pretend to myself that this is him asking me on a date.

"Okay. Bye, Parker. See you tomorrow!" he says before running back down the hall.

"Bye, Liam."

Mom comes running from the kitchen as we walk into the house. "My poor baby!" she cries out and holds me so tight I can barely breathe again. "Are you okay?" I can only nod as the blood rushes to my hurting head. She lets go and looks at me from an arm's length. She looks as if she's searching for more wounds, and I stare back at her while still holding the bag of ice. It's more like water now, actually. "Okay," she says, accepting my current state of health.

I start walking into the kitchen as they talk behind me, thinking I can't hear.

"What happened?" she asks Dad.

"I'll tell you later," he replies.

In the kitchen, Dad takes out the tub of ice cream while I fall onto the couch. This is a mistake, because it makes my head hurt more, but it feels good to lie down. "Parker?" I hear him ask. I mumble something. "Do you want ice cream?"

"Maybe later, Dad."

After that, everything's a blur until the weekend.

Rugby. Why make a kid who's bad at playing football, play it backwards? I don't know. But that's what we did that gym class in Grade 8. By this time, I knew I had major feelings for Liam. And I knew they weren't going away anytime soon, because I thought about him constantly. During school. At the dinner table. Doing homework. Brushing my teeth. Trying to fall asleep. And it was worse when I was around him, because everything was so much more visual and clear. And it was hard not to dream about his eyes, or his hands, or kis—

"Parker!"

I heard someone yell my name and snapped back to reality just in time to see a rugby ball aiming straight for me.

I wasn't quick or athletic enough to catch that ball, though, and it hit me right in the chest. Apparently, I was supposed to do something with it, because a herd of crazy eighth graders were headed straight for me.

So I picked up the ball and ran, in no particular direction, as fast as I could. It was a cool spring afternoon, but it was hot on that field. Suddenly the roar of people grew behind me, and I was tackled to the ground while losing the ball at the same time. Someone picked up the ball, and they all kept running, except for whoever was still on me.

I turned over on the grass to find Liam on top of me, staring into my soul with the eyes that I'd dreamt about the night before, and I wanted nothing more than to kiss him on that field. With everyone watching. I didn't care. But instead of tasting him, he got off me and then pulled me up too.

"Why are you so good at this game?" I asked.

"I'm not. I just follow everyone else and then tackle people," he said with a laugh.

People.

Meaning plural.

———————

On the Saturday before we leave, Liam and I ride our bikes to Stanley Park. We ride down trails through the forests and on the paths along the ocean. I squint at the sparkling water as the smell of the ocean wafts up to us. In the forest, we burn down the trails made by so many people before us.

We pass mossy trees, and I think about what those trees must witness. They see new life growing every spring and new love from people on first dates holding hands. They see the sun set and the sun rise. They see the moon when it's full and when everyone else is asleep. They feel the rain and the snow and the humidity. They get to watch themselves fall apart in the fall and then start new life in the spring all over again. I make a mental note to plant a tree with Liam this summer.

We lock our bikes up and sit on a hill. Liam pulls a piece of grass from the earth and concentrates on peeling it as I stare out at the ocean and count the boats out on the water in the distance. The ocean is my favourite part about living here. It's the perfect place to sit if you need to think or just get away. I ended up coming here a lot last year when I wanted to be by myself and think.

The breeze feels cool on my arms, and it blows my hair around a little. I close my eyes and breathe it in. I'm glad I'm here with him. Ever since we became friends in seventh grade, Liam and I have been inseparable.

He holds out his hand. The air picks up the pieces of grass and takes them away. Then he lies down on his back and closes his eyes, as the sun beats down and paints him golden. I watch him for a while and then look back at the ocean. "What did Mrs. Sharpe say to you?" Liam asks with closed eyes.

"We talked—or rather *she* talked—about different art schools I should think about. You?"

"Same, but for music."

"I guess that means that we won't always have each other," I say.

"We'll always have each other, Parker," he reassures me. There's absolutely no doubt in his voice. I smile at him as he looks up at me with those eyes and then I go back to staring out at the water. I start dividing grass strand by strand like he did. "Parker?" he says after a while.

"Yeah?"

"Do you still think about death?"

I let go of the strands and run my fingers through the soft, dry grass in front of me. "Death?"

"Yeah."

"I don't know. I guess sometimes."

"Like you used to?"

I shake my head. "No, not like that."

He smiles a sweet smile. "Good."

"What about you?" I ask. "Do you think about death?"

"Sometimes."

"Like that?"

He shakes his head too. "No, not like that."

Thank goodness.

"So, what do you think about?" I ask him.

"I don't know. Like when I'll die. Or how I'll die. Or where I'll be when it happens."

"Do you think about it a lot?"

"Not really, just sometimes. Do you ever think about things like that?"

I'm quiet for a beat. "I guess so. But not a whole lot. I think about other things."

"Like what?"

"Like this moment."

His eyes squint tighter as he smiles in the sun. Then he sits up and looks out at the ocean with me.

Five

I've been to my grandparents' acreage about six times. We usually go in the summer and around Christmas time, but we're going in March this year because my parents are going to be busy during the summer. My grandparents are Dad's parents, and they're really nice. They've always tried to get to know me over the years, but they don't know that I'm gay. My parents say it's up to me to tell them, which I love them for, but I don't know how or when I will. My grandparents are conservative Catholics, and my parents aren't sure how they'll react to finding out. I think they just want to protect me for as long as they can.

I'm stoked for this trip, though. I love being out in the fresh country air. This is my first trip with Liam that isn't a field trip, and I'm excited to show him the lake and the orange trees. I feel safe, being four hours away from Dylan and one seat away from Liam.

About an hour and a half into the drive and we're getting close to Hope, BC. We've had to stop three times already, because Liam drinks too much water. When we're on our way again, Liam asks me if I want to play the car game. The basic idea, if you don't know, is that everyone picks a colour and when that colour car passes on the road, you yell it out and get a point. It can go on for hours and get boring, but it's a way to pass the time.

"Okay. I call blue," I say.

"I'm red," he says.

"Mom, what are you?"

She thinks about this for a second, really considering her choice. "I'll be white," she finally decides.

"Dad?"

"Green."

"There are no green cars," I say.

"Green," he says proudly as a green van passes us. That worked out really well for him.

The game doesn't last very long. It isn't even ten minutes before we're all bored and don't even bother to call out our colours. Liam and Dad start talking about the hockey game last night and what all the players did wrong to make us lose. They're really into it, and I tune them out quickly. The farther we drive down the highway, the more mountains and forest we pass on either side of us. It's so breathtakingly beautiful on this bright sunny day, and everything is bathed in light. Liam and I take pictures the whole time. Mom paints her nails in the front seat, and we roll down the windows to let the new spring breeze in and take away the smell of the polish.

Another hour into the drive, my parents are talking to themselves and Liam is passed out against the window. I lean up against my own pillow on the window and watch the rolling hills and mountains pass me by.

———————

I found it in my dad's toolbox by accident. It had held no importance when I'd seen it before. But when I held it then, I knew it would come in handy one day. I didn't think Dad would miss it too much, so I took it. I just slipped it out of its plastic holder and took it up to my room with me. It sat in my drawer, and I thought about it every day.

My parents had both gone to work early one morning, leaving me home by myself until time to leave for school. I thought about what Dylan would do to me that day. It made me sick. I paced around my room, opened the window, and knelt on the floor. My heart was racing. I felt trapped and hot. I needed something to take away the pain I felt in my head.

My eyes were drawn to the dresser. It was sitting in there against my jeans. I could feel it taunting me. I got up and paced around my room some more. I couldn't take it. I opened my drawer and held it. It seemed sharper that day than when I'd first found it.

I sat on the floor and pulled up my sleeves. I traced the blade lightly over my wrist a few times. Then I closed my eyes and began digging it into my skin. It was cold as I dragged it across. A tiny bit of blood slowly trickled down my arm. It hurt so bad I could barely breathe. But I did it again and again. They weren't deep cuts. Nothing that long sleeves wouldn't hide from my parents.

Then without warning, my bedroom door flew open. Terrified, I quickly dropped the razor behind me and opened the bottom drawer, pretending to look for something while I wiped away tears. To this day, I don't know why I didn't just put the razor back in the drawer. But I was panicked. Besides, if I had, this never would have happened.

Liam walked into my room, smiling as usual. "Hey, there you are. What are you doing? We're gonna be late for school," he said.

I rummaged through the drawer and pulled down my sleeves before he could see my wrists. "Sorry, I slept in," I told him.

"What are you looking for?" he asked.

"Nothing," I said. And then without being able to control it, I sniffled. Why did I have to sniffle? I was hoping he wouldn't care about a small thing like that, but he did.

"Are you getting sick?" he asked. I could hear the swooshing noise of him opening and closing the door in a fast motion behind me.

I shook my head. I still wasn't looking at him. "No."

His concern started to grow after that. "Are you okay?" he asked. "You seem kind of strange this morning."

"Yeah," I said, turning around and closing the drawer. "Couldn't find it," I said and shrugged about the thing I'd been pretending to look for.

I noticed he was looking at me strangely, but I couldn't look at him for very long before I turned my attention to the carpet. "Okay ..." he said warily. I started to walk over to the door, when he unexpectedly started coming towards me. "What's that on the floor?" he asked.

Oh. My. Goodness.

I was caught. I could feel it. Why else would it be sitting on my floor? He knew I didn't do any art with that kind of tool. It belongs in the toolbox in the garage anyways.

I tried to stop him. "Liam, please," I said, trying to hold him back.

He pushed past me and picked it up, as I held my breath. I thought I could still see glimmers of red hanging off the edge. "What are you doing with a razor blade?" he questioned me. I couldn't say anything. I was scared and humiliated. I wasn't ready for this interrogation. I hadn't thought it would ever come to this. "Parker," he said sternly, not taking his eyes off me. I was looking around the room, trying to figure out what to say. "Parker! This is serious!" he said even more firmly this time. And the way he said serious let me know he knew what I was doing.

"Nothing, Liam. Let's just go," I said, brushing it off.

"Let me see your arms," he said.

"No, come on."

"Do you really think I'm stupid, Parker? Let me see your arms!" he demanded. I didn't move. He put the blade in his pocket, walked over to me, and pulled up my sleeves. The cotton rubbing against the cuts hurt, and I winced at the pain. He looked down in horror at my left arm, and his mouth gaped. "Oh my gosh ... Parker."

"It's not a big deal," I said, trying to move this along so we could get out of there.

"You call this not a big deal? What's wrong with you!" I pulled my arm away from him and looked at the floor. "I'm sorry. That came out wrong," he said. "Parker, what are you doing to yourself? You know people die from doing this."

"I know."

"Are you trying to kill yourself?"

I started really thinking about whether or not I wanted to. At the time, I thought I could've. It would've all ended. All the pain I took from Dylan. All the nights I lay in bed crying myself to sleep. And high school was next year. Four more years. I didn't want to live another four years of hell. "It's too hard, Liam!" I started yelling. "I can't live with what he puts me through! I can't!"

"I know, but it'll be okay. It'll get better," he said.

"But what if it doesn't get better! Then what?" I continued yelling at him.

"You're so selfish, Parker!" he yelled back. "You're only thinking about yourself. What about me? Do you really think I can live without you?"

I had never thought about what it would be like for him. "This isn't about you," I said decisively.

"Yeah, you're right. When you kill yourself, it won't affect me at all. Or your parents."

That one hit me.

I sighed. "I wasn't going to kill myself," I told him. It was the truth that day. I wasn't going to kill myself that exact morning. But of course it didn't stay the truth for very long.

"Then what are you trying to do?"

I looked down at the floor. It was the only view where I didn't have to see his worried eyes. "I'm just trying to make the pain stop," I told him. "I just want to get away."

"Then let's get away! Let's bike as far away from here as we can and hide every day until we don't have to anymore." He looked at me with sad, tear-filled eyes and then spoke softly. "Parker, I thought we both knew that as long as we had each other, nothing else mattered. Dylan's a loser. We know that now."

I looked up at him. "I'm sorry."

"You have to tell your parents. They can get you help."

"I don't need help," I told him defensively.

"Parker ..." he said, unconvinced that I had this covered.

"I know!"

"If you don't stop ... I'll tell your parents." He paused for a moment. "If you keep doing this to yourself ..." He struggled with the words. "I can't watch you destroy yourself, Parker. I just can't."

We stood there for a while, neither one of us saying anything, and then he stepped closer and hugged me. My head fit perfectly on his shoulder as I hugged him back. "Promise me you won't do this again. Please. Promise me you won't," he begged.

"Okay," I whispered, submitting to his plea.

That hug lasted longer than any other hug between us. If he wasn't going to let go, I wasn't going to either.

"Why did you come here?" I finally asked, realizing I hadn't asked him earlier. We usually just met outside, even if we were late.

"You have my science book," he said.

That was all it took for us to start smiling.

————

I wake up in the car to Liam nudging me in the ribs with his elbow.

"Wake up, sleepyhead," I hear Mom say as I open my eyes and realize where I am. I mumble something. "Are you getting out?" she asks.

"Yeah," I say.

I look over at Liam to see him smiling at me. *Man, I love his smile.* "Wake up, sleepyhead," he jokes.

We grab our stuff out of the back and walk up the gravel driveway to the front porch, where my grandparents meet us. After my Grandma gives me a big hug and my Grandpa messes up my hair, they turn their attention to Liam. "And you must be Liam," Grandpa says.

"Yes, it's nice to meet you. Thank you for inviting me," he says, smiling shyly.

He has so much charm.

"Oh my, such a polite boy," Grandma remarks, making him blush. "We're happy to have you."

After introductions, Liam and I follow Grandma into the kitchen for iced tea. "You're getting so big," she says to me.

I laugh, because I'm actually pretty small for my age, and I don't think I've grown a whole lot since the last time she saw me. But I guess it is different for someone who doesn't see you all the time. "Yeah, I'm huge," I say sarcastically and it makes her laugh.

My grandparents live in an old house on five acres with a porch that wraps all the way around. Their home is probably sixty years old, and every floorboard creaks even when you're trying to be quiet. It's a cozy country house with lots of good hiding places. Years before, my dad would play hide-and-seek with me and I found so many good spots to hide from him. Liam and I don't really play hide-and-seek anymore, but I'll probably still show him.

We join the rest of my family outside. They're sitting in chairs shaded from the sun by a giant umbrella. Mom and Dad already look right at home. Liam and I stand at the edge of the deck and stare out at the never-ending field. "This place is amazing," he says, his eyes never leaving the scenery.

It really is. The sky is free of clouds, and the sun glitters as it reflects into the pool below. Off to the left of the house are orange trees surrounding a gazebo, and beyond that is the vineyard.

We take our bags up to our room. The stairs scream under our weight, and you would have thought we were bears breaking into the house. The third door on the right is Dad's old room from when he was a teenager, and inside everything looks the same as when I was here in December. There are posters of old metal hair bands plastered to the walls, and a lava lamp takes up residence on the nightstand beside the door. One time when we were playing hide-and-seek, I was hiding up here in the closet. Dad took so long to find me that I eventually got bored and started looking around. Deep in the closet, hidden away very purposefully, I found an old tin box that smelled like the back of a van that Liam and I had passed by once, and there were rolling papers inside. When he eventually found me with them, he made up some lame excuse about why they were in there and simply laughed it off. I guess everybody has *something* hiding in their closet. It's funny, because he'd kill me if I ever had the same in mine.

His old bed is neatly made and smells freshly washed. I'm probably a little too eager to share it with Liam. But thinking about the fact that my dad "slept" in it when he was a teenager makes me a little less eager.

Liam's standing by the window looking out into the backyard. I look him over from the bed. His jeans fit snugly, and he's wearing his favourite green Chucks. His hair looks so soft in the light. It makes me wish I could run my fingers through it without it being weird.

I wish he was gay.

I walk over to him and look out. "Do you wanna go explore?" I ask.

"Sure!" he says so enthusiastically it makes me jump a little.

Downstairs, I close the patio door as we walk out onto the deck again. "I'm gonna take Liam exploring," I tell the adults.

Mom is still relaxing in her chair with her eyes closed and drinking iced tea. She works so hard and never takes time off for herself, so this is her time. She squints at me and smiles. "Okay, have fun, boys," she says.

"He really is getting so big," I hear Grandpa say from behind as we gallop down the steps and onto the grass below.

We sprint across the vast yard as fast as we can, with the

hot sun beating down on us and the breeze running through our hair. Liam has always been faster, so I watch him run in front of me. We make it to the vineyard and dash through rows and rows of red grapes.

When our legs can't move anymore, we collapse on the soft ground and try to catch our breaths. I close my eyes. The smell of earth and life fills the air, and it makes me happy to be alive. I look over at Liam lying beside me with his eyes closed, and he makes me forget about the grapes and the soil and the sun and the wind and the world.

I just want to kiss him.

I want to touch his face and his warm skin and run my hands through his hair. I just want to know what it would be like. But it makes my heart hurt, so I look up at the sky and close my eyes instead.

What Liam didn't know about the day he found me cutting myself in my room, was that I did plan to kill myself. Not that day. But one day. I'd lied to him and told him I didn't want to kill myself, because he would've told my parents, and they would've tried to get me help, and I didn't want to talk to anyone about my problems.

It wasn't fair. I just wanted to be a normal kid. I hated feeling sad and scared all the time. I hated having to watch my back every second of the day in case Dylan decided to attack while I wasn't looking. I loved Liam for protecting me, but it was not his job. And the feelings I felt for him I knew would never be reciprocated. It hurt so much to know that the boy I knew I'd love for the rest of my life would never love me back the same way. That was the worst feeling.

I've tried getting over Liam. I really have. But every time I try to force myself into liking someone else, it backfires. I've never met anyone else I can be myself around. Liam is the most amazing person I've ever met, and I feel so comfortable around him. He accepts me for who I am and has never made me feel weird or awkward because I like boys and not girls. He's never accused me of hitting on him or acted strangely around me. Simply put, he's just the greatest best friend I could ever hope for. And more.

But I did have a plan. I didn't feel good about leaving him, but I also felt that I couldn't go on living like that. I knew there was an old bottle of prescription pain pills sitting in my parents' bathroom cabinet, and I could take them after they went to work. When they kicked in, I would slit my wrists and wait. It sounds morbid talking about it now, but at the time, I felt that I had no other choice.

"I'm having so much fun," Liam says and brings me back to the day.

I stay silent for a beat, taking in his voice and his breathing. "Me too."

I'd never had a crush before I met Liam. I've known my whole life that I like boys, but I've never liked anyone the way I like him. Liam has just always been different. Maybe it's because he always seems genuinely happy to be wherever he is. Or maybe it's that smile that melts my heart every time he looks at me and every time I catch him across the room. He has a magnetic personality that lights up wherever we are and draws people to him. He's always listened to me whenever I needed to talk, and I've never felt as if his mind was somewhere else. He makes me laugh when I don't feel like laughing, and he has this sense of comedic timing where he just knows what to say at the perfect time. I don't know how he does it, but it amazes me.

He rolls onto his stomach and starts playing with the dirt. I tilt my head and watch him. He looks serious. That's another thing I like about him. He knows when to be funny and when to be serious. *Not that this is a serious occasion.*

He looks over at me and his eyes dance with the sunlight. "Your grandparents seem really nice," he says.

"Yeah, they are."

He goes back to piling soil in rows. I roll onto my stomach too, put my chin on my hands in front of me, and look into the distance. I hope I end up with someone like him.

After a while, I ask him if he wants to go for a swim. He says he does, so we get up, dust ourselves off, and begin our walk back to the house.

Inside our room for the week, we unpack our stuff a little, mostly just looking for shorts. I meet him downstairs after he's finished changing. Mom insists on sunscreen, so I'm even paler than I usually am. Liam laughs at my paleness when he walks out. "You're next," I laugh back at him. Not that it's any use, he doesn't look any paler after he puts it on.

We run down the steps and scream before splashing into the pool. I kick off from the bottom and gasp for air when I reach the surface. The cool water feels so good on the hot day. Liam swims around me near the edge of the pool, like a shark circling its prey. *I won't mind if you decide to attack*, I think.

After I splash water at him, he sucks air into his lungs and holds it underwater. I begin to circle him now. I learned to swim in this pool the first summer I came here, but I'm still too cautious to go under the water for a long time. He comes bursting out of the water, smiling, laughing, and gasping for air. "Pretty good," I tell him.

"Bet you couldn't do it longer," he teases after he can breathe again.

"Oh, I think you're right," I say back, and we laugh.

We swim until the sun begins to set and the sky becomes pretty with different colours. We race each other from one side to the other and beat each other with inflatable water animals before Mom calls us to dinner.

"So, Parker," Grandpa says halfway through dinner, "how's school?"

"It's okay," I say with a shrug.

He nods approvingly and then looks at me mischievously. "Do you have a girlfriend?"

I choke a little with surprise and feel my face start to turn red, as I look up at him and force myself to smile a little. "No," I tell him. I can feel Liam burning a hole through my head, but I ignore him and turn my focus to my lap.

My grandparents smile and laugh inoffensively at my awkwardness, "What about you, Liam?" he asks.

"No, sir," Liam says.

I've always wondered why Liam doesn't have a girlfriend. Most, if not all, of the girls in our grade practically faint in the halls when he walks by. As I said before, he's gorgeous.

"Well," Grandpa says, "school must be too important then, right?"

"Right," we say simultaneously.

I can still feel him staring at me. While the rest of them talk about gardening and the weather, I give Liam a look that begs him not to say anything. Judging by the look he returns to me, he understands, and I breathe a sigh of relief.

After we rinse off our dishes and put them in the dishwasher, Liam and I go upstairs to change. I feel relieved to get out of there for a while. I hate that question. I never know what to say, and I don't want to say the truth yet. I know I can't lie to them my whole life, though. Eventually I'll reach the age when a girlfriend is simply assumed. And I'm getting really close to that age. Eventually, they will find out. I'm just afraid of what will happen when they do. The church doesn't always accept people like me, and if they're a part of the church, why would *they*?

I walk over to the bed and have just started going through my bag when Liam shuts the door. "Your grandparents don't know you're gay?" he asks.

I turn around to face him. "No."

"Why not?"

"I don't know. I guess there's just never a good time to tell someone that."

"I guess. But your parents are so open-minded; wouldn't they be, too?"

"It's different with my grandparents." I look around the room. "They're from a different generation." My gaze settles back on him. "I don't think they'd understand."

"What about your dad being a vegetarian? Didn't they accept that?"

"Not at first."

"But wouldn't you feel better if you just told them and got it off your chest once and for all?"

"I don't know, maybe. What's with all the questions?"

"I'm sorry. I was just curious."

"What would you do? You know, if you were me?"

He thinks about this for a while and then says, "I don't know. I guess I'd probably do the same." The room suddenly becomes even quieter as we stand around in silence for a moment. Then Liam asks, "Do you like *anyone* at school?"

I turn around and grab what I need from my bag. "No. No one." My heart hurts as I force these words out instead of the ones I want to tell him. "I'm gonna go shower," I say as I squeeze past him and leave the room.

In the bathroom, I lock the door and stand in front of the mirror. Once my hoodie is in the corner on the floor, I rub my arms to try to make the shivers go away. Then I get the shower started and sit on the edge of the tub. The steam rises up, and I begin to feel warm again on the outside.

The water is so hot it burns, but I want it to. I close my eyes and stand under the pressure. Why do I like someone who is never going to like me back? Why do I put myself through this?

"You only won because we forfeited," Liam told Dylan in my bedroom.

"If you guys wanted to win, you could have kept playing," he said back.

"We played for five straight hours!"

I watched them argue back and forth on my bed, while they unrolled sleeping bags and punched pillows in my room. It was the first sleepover I'd ever had at my house. They came over after school and Dad made his "famous" veggie pizza. We watched movies and played video games the whole time. I'd never laughed so hard and had so much fun in my life.

"Besides, it's three in the morning, and I'm tired," Liam continued.

"Whatever," Dylan said jokingly, pulling clothes out of his bag.

"You're so quiet," Liam said to me.

"I'm just tired. You people wear me out," I said and smiled at them.

Liam laughed and pulled off his shirt. Suddenly I felt strange. This was the moment the butterflies moved in. They started flying around in my stomach, as I tried not to stare. It was difficult, though, because I was so attracted to his body. He swiftly replaced the shirt with a new white one. It fit perfectly on his skinny frame. "Yeah, we'll do that. If it wasn't for Dylan cheating, we might have had a real chance to win," he said in Dylan's direction.

"I don't cheat," Dylan said in defence. "I just know how to play."

Liam made a face at me that said Dylan was crazy, while I pretended to move stuff around on my nightstand. Dylan took his shirt off too, but I didn't feel the same way looking at him. I pulled myself together, walked over to my dresser, and took out some clothes. From the corner of my eye, I watched as Liam's hands undid his jeans button, and then I had to leave the room.

When the bathroom door was locked, I sat on the floor, running my hands through my hair and holding my stomach. I'd never felt this way before, and the fact that I didn't know what to do with these feelings scared me. I got dressed, the whole time knowing that I wouldn't sleep that night anyways.

Dylan was passed out on the floor in his sleeping bag by the window when I walked back into my room. Liam was sitting up in his sleeping bag, reading Wringer. He looked up at me as I walked in. It sent shocks all through my body, and I tried hard to act as if I felt normal.

Sitting on my bed and looking down at him, it was as if I were looking at a different person. As if I had never known him before and was finally seeing him for the first time. I noticed his deep blue eyes and how his dark hair fell around his face. I noticed how he sat and how he breathed—silently, but I could hear it now. Nothing else in the world made a sound.

When he looked back up at me, I couldn't look away. And I felt so stupid for just staring at him, but he smiled at me. "This is one of my favourite books," he said.

"Mine too." It took all the strength I had, and when I'd said it, I felt entirely deflated.

"I've probably read it fifteen times."

"Me too." I couldn't come up with anything else to say, but I felt that I had to say something. I looked over at Dylan. "He sure fell asleep fast."

Liam laughed. "Yeah, Dylan's like a toddler: you just have to tire him out and he'll sleep the whole night."

"How long have you been friends?" I asked.

He laughed again. "Since preschool. That's how I know his sleep patterns."

He put the book on my table, sunk deep into his sleeping bag, and closed his eyes. I watched him for a second longer and then got under the covers and stared at the ceiling, thinking about how fast this had happened. An hour ago, he had been just another guy on my couch playing video games, and now he was so much more.

"'Night, Parker," he said below me.

I felt my heart rate increase. "'Night, Liam."

When I walk back into the room, Liam is sitting on the bed. I sit down beside him. "I'm sorry about before," he says.

I look down at the floor. "I'm sorry, too."

"It's just that we don't really talk about it."

"What's there to talk about?"

"I don't know. You never talk about anyone you like, or stuff like that."

"That's because there is no one."

"Okay, well if you ever want to, you can."

I want to. I love you. I dream about you when I'm awake and sleeping. I watch you from the corner of my eye. I need you. When you're gone, I miss you. I want to touch you. I want you to touch me. You're the only one. I can't breathe around you. I can't speak around you. I can't think around you. You captivate me. You thrill me. You fascinate me. Love me back. Don't leave me. You make me feel alive when I'm dying. You save me.

I don't say any of these things.

"Okay, thanks."

I hate lying to him. I want to tell him it's him and it's been him forever. But I want him to feel the same way, and that is a dead dream. I might as well save myself the humiliation and awkwardness and hope that I just get over him.

"I'm gonna take a shower," he says, standing up and grabbing his bag.

"Okay."

*   *   *

"Towels?" Dad asks.

We're standing by the open trunk in the driveway, and he's calling out words on his list. "Check," I say.

"Sunscreen?"

"Check," Liam says as he elbows me in the ribs.

"Ow!" I cry as he laughs.

"Umbrella?"

"Check."

"Shovel and pail?"

"We're not six, but yes, check," I say.

"Water?"

"Yes! Check! Can we please go?" I plead.

I am six years old.

Liam is about to fall apart laughing at me, when Mom comes up from behind and wraps her arms around me. "This is what happens when you stay up half the night," she says jokingly and kisses my head.

"Okay," Dad says. "We can go. But if we're missing anything, we all know who to blame."

It's hot when we get to the beach, and I can't wait to plunge into the water. We race each other to the lake and splash in. The water is cool and sparkling in the sun. We swim while my parents and grandparents sit on the beach and become paparazzi, taking stalker-ish pictures of us.

"I told you it was a good idea," Dad says proudly when we're back on land.

I roll my eyes at him as I bring the shovel and pail over to Liam in the sand. He's already started building the moat around our future sandcastle. "Nice moat," I say.

"Thanks!" he beams.

I scoop some sand into the pail and pack it in tight, then quickly flip it over on the sand near one edge of the moat. After three more, I make walls in between them. Liam uses a stick and carves out little windows in each of the towers and an opening in one of the walls. Some twigs become the bridge.

Later in the day, while lying on the warm sand, I watch my parents sitting and talking in their chairs under the umbrella. I've never met two people more perfect for each other.

They met in university when Dad was twenty-five and Mom was twenty-one. Mom says it wasn't love at first sight for her, but for Dad it was. He says that as soon as he saw her on her first day in the hall he knew he would marry her. But Mom was new to the school, and she was independent and focused on earning her business degree and not dating. That didn't stop Dad, though. He left notes in her locker and would meet her after class and offer to carry her books, the way guys did way back when. He's old fashioned like that. After he'd pursued her for weeks, she finally agreed to go out with him. Mom says he picked her up from her dorm in his car, took her to see a play, and then they went to the fanciest restaurant he could afford.

Dad says the moment he knew that she really was the one

was when they were in the restaurant and she kept looking around awkwardly. He asked her if there was something wrong, and she explained that she wasn't used to being in such a fancy place. He told her they could leave and go wherever she wanted to go, so she suggested a little diner on the corner. He says her face could have lit the whole restaurant when she took a bite of her burger.

By the end of the year, they were in a serious relationship. They talked on the phone every night and spent entire weekends together. That's as much information as they'll give me about that, though. That year was Dad's last year. He had been studying architecture for the last four years, and he was finally graduating. Mom still had another year. They were devastated about not seeing each other every day, and they both say it was one of the hardest struggles they ever went through. They promised that they would see each other every weekend and really make it count. They think I don't know what that means, but I obviously do.

When Dad started working at the same architectural firm he's with today, he rented an apartment close to the campus so they wouldn't be so far away from each other. They say the next year was the longest year of their lives.

We've done the math and discovered that the same year they started dating was the year I was born. Dad calls it crazy. Mom calls it fate.

"Parker!" Grandpa says in alarm, "What happened to your arms?"

I look down at my slashed wrists on the sand and freeze, not knowing what to do or what to say. I look up at Dad for help and see Mom looking at him with the same face.

"The neighbour's cat," Dad covers quickly. "Parker loves to play with it, but it scratches people."

"Oh, I see," Grandpa says, believing the story. "It must be quite vicious."

"Well, at least girls *like* scars on boys, right?" Grandma adds with a smile.

"Right," I say softly, looking up at Dad. He looks relieved that they believe him. I hate lying to them, though, and I know he hates it too. Liam's staring at me when I look over, and I hate that he has to witness us lying because of my actions.

When we're in bed later on, I apologize to Liam for lying to my grandparents. He was so exhausted from the beach he slept the whole way back to the house. Even now, I can tell he's struggling to stay awake.

"It's okay. Everyone lies," he says softly.

"Yeah, right! When have you ever lied?"

"I don't know, but I have; everyone does. We can't help it."

"I guess."

I'm glad that that awful moment wasn't the time that they found out about me.

I don't want this week to end. I don't want Liam to go back to his own house, and I really don't want to go back to school.

"Liam?" I ask.

No answer. Either he's fallen asleep or he's ignoring me. I decide it's the first, throw off the covers, close my eyes, and try to forget that his body is beside mine. I think about my parents instead and how well they fit as a couple. Dad will do anything to make Mom laugh and see her smile. Sometimes I observe them when they watch TV together or when they read the paper in the morning. They sit on opposite sides of the table with their sections of the paper and they know exactly when to switch with each other without saying a word, and I smile at them from behind my toast. I've only known them for almost five years, but they're my whole world. I don't know what I'd do without them.

Six

The next day it doesn't just rain, it pours. Raindrops the size of dimes come crashing to the ground. Liam and I are sitting on the living room floor watching the showers through the window. If we were home, we'd be outside already, biking through the neighbourhood or maybe to the stables just south of the city where we once learned how to ride horses. That didn't work out, though, with the horses. I kept falling off mine, and Liam's horse hated him. But our tradition is halted while we're here with my grandparents.

"It's never going to stop," I say to him.

"It might," he says half-optimistically. "Or we could go outside anyways."

Try not to picture him soaking wet right now, I tell myself. Unfortunately, I can't. "My grandma would probably say we would catch a cold," I say.

"Yeah," he says with a sigh. We both return to looking at the rain-drenched front lawn.

"It's not much fun, is it?" Dad says as he and the rest of the adults join us in the room.

I shake my head. "Not really."

Grandma sits in a chair and says, "There's a trunk in the basement filled with old clothes and costumes if you boys would like something to do."

I think about this for a second. I'm not really in the mood for dressing up, and they'll probably take pictures that will haunt me the rest of my life.

Dad says, "Or you can stay up here with the old people while we talk about politics and weather."

Suddenly costumes don't seem so bad. I look over at Liam and he's pleading with me with his eyes.

The stairs groan as we walk down into the dark basement. The lighting casts shadows that look like figures against the walls as we duck under cobwebs and choke on the dust that floats in the air. We make our way around slowly through what seems like hundreds of century-old boxes.

Eventually Liam says, "I think I found it." He's standing beside a sewing mannequin and moving boxes around. I walk over and eye the mannequin suspiciously. I don't know which is creepier, one with a head or one without. I push it off to the side and watch it rock back and forth before it stops. "Can you grab that side?" he asks.

He's holding one handle of the trunk off the ground. I stop looking at the fabric human and take the other handle as we pull it out into an open space.

When he opens the lid, we start coughing uncontrollably as all the dust flies out and settles in the air. He starts going through the old clothes, and he looks as if he's having a lot of fun. "What do you think?" he says, putting on a flowery hat.

"I don't know. I don't think it's your colour," I say. I rummage through the box, pull out a straw hat, and put it on his head. "Yes. Definitely the straw hat," I tell him.

He smiles, "I need a piece of wheat to chew on now."

"Maybe if we were in Alberta," I say. "But we could possibly get some hay from the neighbour's farm."

"Really?" He looks at me with huge wonder-filled eyes. It's hilarious seeing him this excited about dressing up, and I can't help but laugh at him.

"Yeah, maybe when it stops raining, or tomorrow, or something."

"Okay, you need something too," he says.

"Like what?"

He starts searching through the box, pulling clothes out and putting them in piles on the floor, trying other hats and necklaces on, and wrapping scarves around my neck. "Here!" He pulls out a pair of tattered brown cowboy boots. "Try them on!"

I laugh at him and pull them on. They actually fit perfectly, and Liam decides it was meant to be.

"Can you walk in them?" he asks

We laugh as I wobble to the end of the room. On the turn around, a stack of black and white photos catches my eye, and I check them out. Liam walks over in his straw hat as I take out a pile. We sit on the floor, sifting through them.

They're dated back to September 1951. My grandparents are in them, and they look to be in their twenties. Most of them are taken at a football game with friends. In a couple of photos, they're sitting side by side in a diner drinking a milkshake. They're the kinds of pictures you see in movies but not actually ones you know about.

"These are pretty cool," Liam says.

"Yeah, they are," I say, flipping through.

"It looks like it was a fun time back then." I nod, but I don't say anything. I'm thinking about my own family history and how I'll never know what it is. He must have read my mind and known something is wrong because he says, "What are you thinking about?"

"I'm not related to them," I tell him honestly.

He thinks about something for a beat and then says, "Maybe not by blood, but you are by love."

I've never heard him say anything so beautiful. "Thanks, Liam," I say.

I look over at him and suddenly our faces are so close. Like really close. So close that it wouldn't be difficult at all to lean in and kiss him.

"Are you boys hungry?" Dad shouts from the top of the

stairs. We jump. *How long has he been there? And what just happened?*

He walks down the creaky stairs and over to us. "Nice cowboy boots," he says.

I look up at him and laugh. "Oh, thanks."

"I wore those for Halloween a couple years."

"Really?"

"And before that they were your grandpa's when he was around your age."

"He really wore those?" Liam asks excitedly.

"Sure did," Dad says.

"That's awesome!" Liam exclaims. I look over at him. I love that he loves the little things.

And about whatever that moment was, whatever I wanted to happen, it's gone. I have to remember that. Liam is just my best friend. That's all.

"Yeah, he was quite the fashionable kid back in his day. I remember looking at pictures of him when I was your age. They're in one of these boxes ..." He fades off somewhere for a second and then comes back. "Your grandma made cookies. They're in the kitchen," he says before messing up my hair and walking away.

Putting the pictures back in the box, I take one last look at the people sitting in the booth together and think about what Liam said.

Around three in the afternoon, the showers finally stop and the sun starts to dry up most of the puddles. All six of us are playing Monopoly on the living room floor. Liam's new hat was a hit with everyone and we got tons of funny pictures.

"Seems like the rain's stopped for now," Dad says as I look up from buying Pacific Avenue.

"Does that mean we can go outside?" I ask.

He looks over at Mom, and I watch her nod. "Sure," she says.

"Thank you!" I say, standing up. "Come on, Liam."

He looks up at me from his spot on the floor. "But I'm

winning," he says with an exaggerated half-frown, half-smile.

"You can win another time; you always win, anyways." He looks back at the board and then up at me. "Outside!" I say, trying to persuade him.

He smiles at me and gets up reluctantly. "Okay ..."

I stop halfway to the door and turn around. "Can I wear these outside?" I ask, pointing to the boots I'm still wearing.

"Sure! Have fun!" Dad says as Liam joins me by the door with his hat.

"So about this farm ..." Liam says slyly as we run down the steps and turn right onto the lawn heading towards the vineyard.

I laugh at him. "It's this way!"

We run through the orange trees and the vineyard and finally make it to the neighbour's property. They have cows, horses, and chickens, and they have hay bales beside the barn. We aren't really supposed to be on their property, so we have to be quiet and careful. Of course, this makes it so much more fun.

We peek over and then climb to the other side of the tall wood fence and stealthily creep our way towards the barn. No one is in sight, so they're probably inside. I almost slip in the mud a couple times because the boots have no grip. The barn is on the far side of the field, so we have to run and hide behind chicken coops in order to stay out of view.

"We're so close," I say, laughing from behind the second coop. "Okay, run!"

We run out from behind and gallop across the field. We're almost to the barn when I lose my balance on a slippery patch of mud and fall onto my back on the slick wet grass. The blue sky becomes my focus. Liam stops and reaches his hand out. "Are you okay?" he asks.

I sit up and smile at his concerned face. "Yeah," I say, laughing and taking his hand.

We run the last couple of steps as I brush the rest of the mud off my jeans. When we're out of sight, we sit on the hay bales and gasp for breath while laughing so hard it hurts. "Okay, which one do you want?" I ask, gesturing to the bales.

He looks intensely at them all, pulls out a couple pieces of hay, and puts one in his mouth. He puts the rest in his back pocket. I give him a strange look. "In case we get hungry," he says, and we burst out laughing.

I can hear water rushing from behind the forest. "Come on," I say to him.

We take off again, climbing the back fence and running through the trees, ducking under branches and watching out for holes in the ground. I lead him to the river that runs behind the forest. Dad and I usually come here when we visit, although we don't usually cut through the neighbour's farm.

We stand by the river and look at it in awe. I turn to Liam as he chews his piece of hay, and he gives me a funny smile. We would probably look so strange to anyone watching: one boy with a straw hat chewing hay and another wearing cowboy boots, just walking along the river.

The river stretches on across from us for a long time, so maybe it's more like a lake. I don't know. There's a tire swing tied to a giant tree that hangs right over the water. Dad says it's been there since he was little. When we came here, we used to swing off it and jump in. It's deep enough for diving off the dock here, but the farther down the path you go the more rapid and dangerous the water becomes.

Liam throws his hat off his head like a Frisbee. It lands softly on the grass behind us. "Do you feel spontaneous?" he asks. I don't know. But next to leave his body is his shirt, and I sure feel *something*. I can't help but stare. "Let's go swimming!" he says.

I don't even have time to think before he's throwing off his shoes, and his jeans drop to his ankles. He runs over to the giant tree in his boxers. I watch him climb the trunk with squirrel-like capability. He pushes himself up onto a branch and walks across, balancing until he reaches the end. He looks down at me and smiles. I smile back. Then he swiftly lowers himself off the branch and down the rope onto the tire.

"What are you doing?" I laugh. I thought I should say something, because I've just been staring at him the whole time, and it's probably getting weird.

He simply smiles back down at me again as he tries to get the swing moving. He leans back and kicks his legs up in order to start the process. After a couple tries of swinging it back and forth, he finally gets a fluid motion and then cannonballs into the river (or lake). After being under the water for a second, he comes up for air and waves me over.

I don't want to be weird, so I strip down and run in.

The water chills me to the bone. Liam swims around in this unbelievably happy state. I hold my breath and go under until only my eyes are above the water, and I watch him. This is a thousand times better than the pool at the house.

Now would be the perfect time to kiss him. I've seen it in movies. It's supposed to be super romantic kissing in water. He swims over. "Hold your breath with me," he says.

I shake my head. Is there a reason I can't make any words? *Probably because I'm in love with him and we're inches apart in the water. Alone.*

"Come on, it's easy," he tells me. "Like this." He smiles before holding his breath and going underwater. He's such a show-off. He comes back up quickly and shakes his head, sending his hair flipping to the side and water spraying everywhere. "See? Just hold your breath and go under! What are you afraid of?"

Everything.

"What if I drown?" I ask.

"I'll save you."

"What if you don't know I've drowned?"

"Parker, you can't drown that quickly. I'd notice," he smirks.

"Okay, fine." I give in.

"Okay! It's easy. Just breathe in and hold your breath." He's waiting for me to do it. "Parker!" He rolls his eyes at me.

Fine, I think. I breathe in as much air as I can and hold it. "Now go under!"

I sink down until I'm completely immersed by the river-lake. But I forgot to close my eyes and the water stings immediately. After a second, the water in front of me ripples in all directions as Liam submerges himself. It's only been three seconds, but it's three seconds too long without air, so I resurface. I hear Liam come back up while I'm rubbing my eyes.

"Parker, don't cry," Liam teases me.

"I got water in my eyes," I tell him.

"Parker, you're supposed to close your eyes!"

"Now you tell me," I say.

He laughs. "Here, let me see." I move my hands away and allow him to look at my water-damaged eyes. He very gently reaches out and touches his fingers to my cheek just under my left eye. I don't know what he's looking for, but I don't think he should stop. I hope I don't look as scared as I feel. "I think you're okay," he says after a moment. He takes his hand away and then swims back a couple of feet with a smile on his face as if nothing happened.

Nothing did happen, I tell myself. *Nothing.*

It seems that time doesn't exist in this part of the forest. *How long have we been swimming? An hour? Maybe more?*

After a while, we walk back over to our clothes on dry land. "That was good, Parker. Maybe next time you'll remember to close your eyes," he says with a chuckle and gently shoves me with his wet hand. I'm so glad I haven't put my shirt on yet, because his hand slips right off my wet shoulder and I know I'll never forget the way that feels.

Once we're dressed, we start walking the same path that runs along the water. Liam abruptly stops a couple of paces behind me and steps onto a wide, flat rock near the riverbank. *We've reached the rapid area,* I think as I join him. We sit down with our knees to our chests and stare out into the forest on the other side. Some water still bleeds through our jeans. Fish swim and jump out of the water in front of us.

Liam puts his chin on his knees and closes his eyes. I watch him, making sure he doesn't lose his balance and fall in. I'm not sure how deep it is on this side, but the current looks pretty strong. "I really love it here," he says, with eyes closed.

I keep watching him. "I do too."

We sit there for a while and talk about life. He talks about his dad getting remarried and how sometimes he wishes his parents were still together, but not all the time.

Liam's parents got divorced last September. His parents met in Ottawa when they were in their early twenties. They were staying at the same hotel and saw each other through the crowded hotel bar. After that, they saw each other a couple more times before Liam's mom flew back to Vancouver and his dad went back to Halifax. A few months later, Liam's mom called him and explained that she was pregnant, with Liam. Liam's dad packed up his life in Halifax and flew literally across the country to be with her. They got married in the winter, after Liam was born, and stayed in the city.

Liam and I were born a week apart. Maybe it was even in the same hospital. Liam's dad worked as an electrician before he bought the company years later, and his mom owns her own cosmetic company. Liam's lived in the same house just around the corner from mine his whole life. He says that every wall has a memory.

They started fighting when Liam was twelve. They fought about money, and Liam's mom suspected his dad of cheating on her. They went to counselling, but after three years of arguing back and forth, they decided to get divorced. It was really rough on him. His parents got joint custody, but his dad agreed that he should live at his mom's, because it's his home.

His whole world caved in on him when he suddenly didn't have his dad around all the time and had to stay at two different houses. But he says that it gets easier and he's gotten used to the way life is now, and he probably wouldn't change it even if he could.

"It's getting pretty late," I finally say. "We should probably head back."

"Yeah, I guess so," he says, standing, stretching, and hopping back onto the grass.

I'm getting up to follow him off the rock, but the boots can't grip the surface and they rapidly slip off, taking me with them. I splash into the water, and I hear Liam scream my name as he tries to grab my hand. But he isn't quick enough, and our hands just graze at the fingertips. I plunge under the water. I'm holding my breath while everything moves around my open eyes. I try to think, but I find it too difficult a task because everything is happening too quickly. Finally, I come up to the surface and gasp for air while flailing my arms and trying to find something to hold onto. I hear footsteps rustling through the tall grass and Liam's voice calling for help before I'm taken down again.

Seven

My eyes open, and I cough up water. I'm lying on the grass with a blanket around my shoulders, and there are people standing around me. One is Liam, two of them have RCMP badges, and a fourth I don't know. I feel chills run through my body. My head and stomach hurt. I feel Liam's hand on my shoulder, and the others are looking at me and talking, but I can't understand what they're saying. I sit up quickly and cough up more water, but that was a bad idea, so I lay back down. "What happened?" I hear myself say.

One of the Mounties speaks, and I can hear him now. "You hit your head on a rock after you slipped into the water. Luckily your friend called for help, and Mr. Buckner pulled you out of the water."

I look over at Liam and then at the man who saved my life. Liam looks terrible, and I think he might cry, but he doesn't. I do, though.

"Thank you," I say to the man, barely able to get the words out. I know it's not enough for what he's done for me, but it's all I have.

"You're very welcome," he says. "You're lucky your friend can scream louder than anyone I've ever known."

I suppose I can thank all the hours he spends singing along

to screamo. Liam doesn't smile. He just remains silent and holds my shoulder. I sit up slowly.

Mr. Buckner continues, "I was fishing just a little ways down when I heard him and started running towards you guys. I saw you floating in the water and quickly pulled you out. Your friend was about to jump in after you, and I had to stop him."

I look at him in shock. "I don't know what to say. You saved my life." I start crying harder when I try to replay the events in my head. "Thank you so much."

"Don't worry about it, kid. I'm just glad I got to you in time." He looks at me for a while with sad eyes. "Just be careful next time."

I nod at him. I'm too choked up to say anything. Liam is still silently kneeling beside me.

The other Mountie speaks now. "We'd better get you kids home. Where do you live?"

I tell him where we're staying, and then we walk down a trail and out to a police car. Before I get in, I look over at Mr. Buckner for a beat. I can't say anything, but he nods as if he understands how much I appreciate what he's done.

When he walks away, I get into the back of the police car with Liam. When we start to drive away, Liam takes my hand in his and I cry on his shoulder.

Mom gasps in horror when she sees me soaking wet standing with Liam and the Mounties on the front porch. Everything happens so fast I don't even know whether words are exchanged. She pulls me towards her and then rushes me inside to our room. Dad stays behind and talks to the RCMP.

Liam and I stand in our room as Mom runs the bathtub. I toss the blanket onto the bed, take off my soaked shirt, and throw it on the floor. I look at him. "Liam," I say.

As soon as I say his name, he breaks down, wraps his arms around me, and cries. He's so warm, and he's exactly what I need. "I was so scared, Parker," he says through his crying. I hug him tight. "I thought …" he starts. "I …" I hug him even tighter, and he knows I know what he's thinking. I'm thinking it too.

Mom opens the door, and we slowly break apart. "Your bath is ready, baby," she says. She looks at me so sadly. There are tears in her eyes as she walks over and hugs us both.

In the bathroom, I lean against the counter and wrap my arms around myself. I'm still trying to figure out how this all happened. When I was in the water, I didn't know whether I would make it back out. I was terrified. I could hear Liam's voice for a while, but I couldn't see him, and then I couldn't hear him anymore. The Mounties checked for bleeding at the back of my head, but they only found a small scratch and said that I should be fine. They think I must've hit my head on a rock underwater and lost consciousness. I look at myself in the mirror. I'm soaking wet. I peel off the rest of my clothes, and they fall with a thump to the floor.

"What does your future look like, Parker?" the psychologist asked me.

I was examining the painting on the wall, trying to figure out what was under all those layers of colours. I turned to him. "I don't know."

"What would you like it to look like?"

"I don't know," I said a little sadly.

"You've never thought about what you would do in the future? Five years from now? Ten years from now?"

"Not really."

He studied me for a while. "Why is that?"

I thought about it for a while. "I think ..." I started to say as my gaze slowly moved across the room and back to the painting. "Sometimes I can't even think to the end of the day ... The future just seems too far away to think about."

In the morning, local news reporters come to the house asking to speak with me, but Grandpa tells them that I'm too weak and exhausted with everything that's happened to answer any questions. He did let them know that I was doing okay, though.

Mr. Buckner got his photo in the paper, with the title Local Hero. Grandma cut it out and pasted it to the fridge after she baked him some of her awesome peanut butter cookies.

I'm too worn out to get out of bed for most of the day, so Liam and I listen to records we found in our room and play card games. Occasionally my parents or my grandparents come and play a round of Go Fish with us. My grandparents had been scared too. I'm not their only grandchild, but I am the only boy, so in a way I think that makes me a little special to them.

I can't believe how fast time has flown by when the next day my parents are starting to pack. It seems like we've just gotten here and I don't want to leave yet. On our last night, we all sit around the fire pit in the backyard and make s'mores. Dad had picked up a bag of vegan marshmallows back in Vancouver just for the occasion.

*   *   *

"Are you ready to go?" Dad asks from the doorframe on our final morning.

I'm finishing the last of my packing on the bed. "Yeah," I tell him.

He walks over to me and sits on the bed. "How's your head?"

"It feels okay."

"Good." I stuff a shirt into my bag. "Are you excited to get back home?"

I look up at him. "No."

He looks at me with sympathy. I get that a lot. "I know times are tough right now, Park, but they'll get better."

I nod and zip up my bag. "Okay, I'm ready."

Liam's already outside hugging my grandparents goodbye. Mom takes my bag when I get near the trunk and I hug them goodbye too. Another visit has come and gone without me telling them. I don't know when I'll do it. Someday, I guess. We wave to them as we pull out of the driveway and head home.

The drive home always seems to go by faster than the journey there. After five stops for Liam and a few more for pictures of mountain goats, we're back in our driveway where it all began, and I'm so tired. We dropped off Liam before going home, and I told him I'll see him on Monday. I need a day to myself to sleep and think about nothing and everything. As soon as I shut my bedroom door, I'm face first onto my bed and then fast asleep.

Eight

It's Thursday, the day before the art contest. I'm sitting on the stairs and thinking about tonight. Tonight can't happen. I know it will whether I like it or not, though. That's the difficult part to accept. But it just can't. I've gotten way ahead of myself here. Let me go back to what happened yesterday.

After classes started again, things at school were going fine—until Dylan punched me in the stomach after PE, that is. I attempted to hide this fact from my parents, but I was found out when Dad asked me to grab a glass from the top shelf of the cupboard. Now, this may seem like an effortless task, but I knew that if I reached for it, the pain in my stomach would inflame, and they'd ask what was wrong. At the same time, I knew that making an excuse for something as simple as grabbing a glass would make me look even guiltier of something.

Mom was cutting up vegetables behind me. Dad was in the dining room, setting the table. I turned to look at each of them carefully before driving one leg up onto the counter and holsting myself onto the surface. Once on my knees, I was able to reach the glass without any added effort. *Success,* I thought.

"What are you doing?" I heard Dad ask. I swivelled quickly on my knees and saw him standing beside me with a puzzled face. Mom turned around too, with knife in hand.

"Getting the glass. Like you wanted," I told him. I wanted to roll my eyes: *obviously.*

"Why did you climb all the way onto the counter?" he asked. Mom wasn't saying anything. I think she knew he was hunting for something. She kept looking back at him and then to me. I tried to keep my cool.

"Why is that so strange?" I asked, handing him the glass.

"Well, it's just that you haven't had to do that in a couple of years." He means one year. But we let ourselves think I've grown more than the few inches I have.

"Didn't think it was a big deal," I said. Proud of myself at how smoothly it had run off my tongue.

He shrugged his shoulders and gave up. The small prey had defeated the hunter. Of course, life is unfair, because as I was getting down, my knee slipped on the counter. I reached out, grabbed hold of the cabinet shelf to catch myself, and felt the stretch in my stomach before letting out a cry of agony. Even without Dylan, I'm simply prone to injury. This time though, I'd just classify it as clumsiness.

Mom twisted around, still holding the knife, and I screamed as she scared me half to death with it just after I had scared her. She put it down just as I found my footing. Dad rushed in too. "Are you okay?" Mom asked.

"Yeah, just slipped," I said trying to brush it off as nothing.

They shared a look between them. "Just be more careful next time," Mom said. They knew something was up as they went back to their tasks, but they weren't going to force it out of me. They didn't have to. As soon as I took a step, it sent unbelievably powerful shocks up my leg to my stomach, and I doubled over in pain, hugging myself tight. Of course, they were on me in a heartbeat and wanted to know what was wrong. I didn't get away with saying *nothing* this time.

So eventually, reluctantly, I told them how Dylan had come up to Liam and me after class and punched me, and I showed them the bruise that was forming under my ribs on my right side.

Their reaction to this game we play used to be outrage. They used to call Mrs. Baker and Mr. Morrison as soon as they found a black eye or a cut somewhere on my face and would call a meeting to get things straightened out. Nothing ever did get straightened out, though. Otherwise we wouldn't still be in the mess, and reaching a glass on the top shelf wouldn't be such a hassle (except for my height, naturally).

But over time their reactions have become less ... fire-breathing dragon-esque. Their anger over the issue hasn't dropped; they've just gotten better at keeping it under control. This is appreciated.

This time was pretty much the same, but it was laced with something else. They were calm, but they were too calm. They almost didn't say a single word in the kitchen, and all throughout dinner they were silent. Completely silent.

After dinner, I escaped to my room and called Liam. After I told him what was happening, he agreed that it sounded strange. After I'd been punched in the hall, Liam had decked Dylan in the jaw and made him bleed. Dylan had swung back at him, but Liam had ducked and Dylan had missed him by inches. Liam had then shoved him to the floor. Dylan had scrambled to his feet just as the bell rang for next class. Before he could do any more damage, Liam had grabbed my hand, and we had taken off running down the hall. We were laughing so hard by the time we got back to our lockers. Then he let go of my hand. I had to keep laughing, so he wouldn't know how much it killed me when his soft skin slipped forever away.

Later that night, just as I walked out of my bedroom to go say good night, Mom yelled up the stairs, "We're having company!"

"When?" I asked as I joined her and Dad in the living room. I stood behind the couch as they turned to me.

"Tomorrow evening," she said. "Mrs. Baker and—"

"Dylan's mom?" I cut her off, suddenly fearful.

"Yes, sweetheart," she said.

My heart started racing. My palms were overwhelmed, tucked inside my hoodie sleeves. "Why?" I asked. "What for?"

"They're going to come over so we can talk," she said.

"They?" I panicked. "*They? Dylan's mom and Dylan?*" I started walking circles in the room. They stared at me as I walked over, opened a window, and then sat on the floor and hugged my knees. "That's not company," I told them. "That's the enemy."

"Parker, it's only going to be for an hour," Dad reassured me as he joined me on the floor.

"That's like forever, Dad," I told him. He smiled sweetly at me, but I was having none of it. "Why?" I asked.

"Because kids like Dylan need to know that they can't treat kids like you this way," he said.

"Kids like me?" I looked up at him. "What does that mean?"

"You know what I mean," he told me.

"No. What do you mean? Shy kids? Small kids? Gay kids? Or how about all of the above? We all know I fit that character to a T."

"Parker," Mom said as she sat beside me. Her voice was calm and soft. But I was having none of that, either. "You know that's not what we meant."

"I don't want this to happen," I told them.

"I'm sorry," Dad said. "It's happening."

I got up and made a beeline for the stairs. "I wish I'd died," I said.

"Parker!" Dad shouted behind me.

I turned to look at them, standing by my open window, letting all the spring air in. "Then none of this would be happening!" I screamed at them and ran up the stairs. I slammed my bedroom door.

So that was yesterday. And now here I am, sitting on the stairs, dreading the moment the doorbell rings. Mom wanted me to get dressed in something nicer, but I told her jeans and a T-shirt was all she was getting. After what they're putting me through, I think it's only fair that I get to decide what I wear.

Mom comes around again and looks up at me. I feel only slightly bad for saying what I said yesterday. You know, about wishing I'd died. But the more she checks on me, the worse I begin to feel. "It won't be so bad, sweetie," she tells me, putting her face up to the banister. I ignore her and continue to stare at the door.

She walks away, and I fix the cuff on my jeans, diverting my attention away from the front door. As soon as I hear the doorbell ring, I bolt up the stairs. But before I get the chance to hide away forever behind my door, Dad catches me and places me firmly back on my feet. From the corner of my frightened eyes, I see Mom going to answer the door. I look away, but I can't look at Dad until he says, "Listen to me, Parker." He looks downstairs as we both watch Dylan and his mom walk into our house. My knees go weak. If Dad wasn't holding me up by my arms, I'd be a puddle on the floor. He gestures to my room, and we escape into the dark while Mom chats downstairs. He still holds me firmly. "Listen," he repeats. "This is only going to take an hour. After that you can run up here and cry all you want before calling Liam." *How does he know me so well?* I think. He goes on, "But right now, you have to suck up any fears you have, walk down those stairs, and join us for a civilized conversation. And I never want to hear you say you wish you were dead again, do you understand? I love you more than life itself. If you died, I'd die too. *Do you understand?*"

I nod. We're both trying our hardest to keep tears locked up behind our eyes.

"Okay?" he asks, his strong voice searching for reassurance.

"Okay," I manage to squeak out.

"Okay." In the moment after he pulls me close and I smell the cologne on his pressed shirt, I feel safe. But I know he can't save me from everything, any more than Liam can. No matter how badly I need him to.

Downstairs, Mom is entertaining Dylan's Mom with a glass of wine. *To ease the tension, perhaps.* They look like friends talking in the kitchen. I feel almost weird about it. "There you are," Mom says when she spots us.

Dad and Mrs. Baker shake hands and say hello. I'm trying hard not to, but my eyes eventually break free and look into the living room. Dylan's sitting in the chair closest to the window. His eyes are fixed on something on the ground. The bruise around his mouth and jaw is really starting to show. I watch him for a while, not able to look away. Just like me, he's wearing the same clothes he wore to school today. Suddenly he looks over at me. His eyes narrow in as he glares. I quickly look away and head deeper into the kitchen, just as Dad says, "Why don't we all have a seat?"

Knowing I won't go willingly, Mom guides me by my shoulders and I squeeze as tightly as I can between the sofa and coffee table to sit between my parents. Mrs. Baker sits closest to Dad in the other chair. There is at least eight feet separating Dylan and me, but it's still not enough for comfort.

Dad is about to speak, when Mrs. Baker says, "I'm so sorry we have to do this again."

At least one of them is, I think.

"We are, too," Mom says.

Dylan and I both remain silent and uninterested in the event of the evening. I occasionally look up at him from the set of coasters on the coffee table, but I look away when he glares at me again. It's hard to believe this is the same Dylan that once sat here with me and laughed while we played video games.

I manage to tune out our parents' conversation and try to think about other things—not Liam, though. I'm afraid Dylan will be able to tell and lunge across the room for my throat. Instead, I think about the art contest at school tomorrow. The school hired an actual panel of judges to come check out our work.

In class today, I put the final touches on my drawing. While cleaning up, I took a minute to look over what some other kids were working on. Todd had made an abstract sculpture made entirely out of coloured toothpicks. He smiled at me when he saw me looking at it, but I turned away.

A few minutes before the bell rang, Liam showed up at the door and came to visit me. Band had ended early and he had nothing to do until we went home. Most teachers object to other students in their classrooms, but Liam could rob a bank with that smile. He teased me about the lack of colour in my drawing because I'm "dark and brooding." I got back at him by streaking a line of charcoal across one of his cheeks. We laughed until the bell rang and then raced each other down the crowded hall, much to the dismay of the worn-out teachers.

"Does that sound okay?" Mom asks from some distant place. I fade back in to find she's still sitting beside me.

Oh, crap. I was thinking about Liam. I look over at Dylan. Could he read it? Was it written all over my face? He cringes as our eyes meet, and I quickly look away.

"Parker?" Mom says. I turn to her. "Dylan would like to apologize. Does that sound okay?"

He wants to apologize? Just like that? Does he *know* how to do that? Who's forcing him to do this unimaginable act? How much time has gone by? I know that no matter how he chooses to say it, it won't be genuine. It won't be coming from him. But I nod anyways. Sure, why not?

Mom smiles. That's followed by more smiles from Dad and Mrs. Baker. Dylan still wears his famous frown. His mom looks over at him, and I watch a silent conversation happen behind their eyes.

Finally, Dylan clears his throat and says, "I'm sorry."

Oh ... so that's what an apology sounds like, I think. I quickly nod and look back to the coasters with their animal faces.

And so the dreaded evening is over. Our parents seem relieved that we've made up and sorted things out. Now they can sleep soundly, knowing they were the ones who made it happen.

As soon as everyone gets up, I hurry out of the room, anxious to get away from this nightmare. But, as I find out at the stairs, the nightmare is apparently just beginning.

On my way up, a hand catches my ankle, forcing me to trip and land on my elbows. I turn around to see Dylan hovering over me. "Don't think this is over," he says in a menacing voice. "You told your parents and got me in trouble. You're gonna pay for this, Parker."

He stares me down with one more glare before turning and walking out the front door. Moments later, Mom and Dad say good night to Mrs. Baker.

"Well, that went okay," Mom says after Dad closes the door.

They both look over at me before I pick myself up, dash up the stairs, and run into my room. They don't come up after me. Because, like Dad said, now I get to cry all I want before calling Liam.

Nine

The art contest starts at seven, but I left around six thirty and biked to school to set up my drawing for the viewing. There are judges walking around right now with clipboards and pens. Looking around the room, I see that all the other drawings, paintings, and sculptures are really good and a lot more creative than mine, so I'm not getting my hopes up on winning. But this is finally my chance to do something where I don't have to be afraid of Dylan, so I'm happy about whatever happens.

"I'd give it first place," I hear Liam say behind me. He's standing with his mom.

"Hey, I'm glad you came," I say.

"Of course. I wouldn't miss this."

"It's very good, Parker," Mrs. Eriksson says.

"Thank you."

"Liam tells me it has a story behind it."

Liam's mom hangs on every word as I tell her the story about my dream, and she seems genuinely interested to hear about it. She wishes me good luck and then they leave to look around at the others. Some more people come over to look at mine and offer their comments, all of which are very generous. After a while, the judges with their clipboards come over. They enquire about what had inspired me and ask some other questions. While they talk to me, I can see my parents standing off to the side, pretending not to watch me. After the judges leave, they come over.

"There's our artist," Dad says.

"We're so proud of you, Parker. Were those the judges who just left?" Mom asks.

"Yeah. I don't know if they liked it or not, though. I couldn't tell."

"Well, we think it's great," Dad tells me.

"Thanks."

Liam comes running over just then and says hi to my parents.

"Hi, Liam. Where's your mom?" Mom asks him.

"She's around here somewhere," he says, out of breath.

"Okay, well, we're gonna go have a look around. We'll come find you when they call the winners," Mom says before they walk away.

"Parker." Liam puts his hand on my wrist and looks straight at me. It ignites something inside me. I have to push that feeling away and then disentangle myself from his grasp.

"What?" I ask.

"Dylan's here."

I feel a knot form in my stomach. Suddenly I want his hand back. "Are you serious?"

"He's here to see his sister's painting," he tells me. My mind freezes. *How could he be here?* I think. "Are you okay?" Liam asks after a second.

"Yeah." But how could I be okay knowing he's so close to me?

Suddenly, a voice comes on the intercom and calls everyone to the stage, but I can't move.

"We'd better head over. Are you okay?" he asks again. I nod as I force myself to move and we walk to the stage, but inside I want to run away.

Ten minutes later, we're standing there in the crowd while the announcer is talking and people are clapping. But I'm not paying attention. I'm trying to look around the room for Dylan, but I'm too short to see over most people. He's in here somewhere, I know. Why did he have to be at the same place as me, just when I felt safe?

People around me start clapping again for something that I've missed, and then Liam painfully jabs me in the ribs. "Parker! You won second place!" he says.

"What?"

"They called your name. Go!"

"Oh." I'm not even focused on the contest anymore. I search the crowd as soon as I get onto the stage, and one of the judges shakes my hand.

"Congratulations, Parker," he says.

"Thank you. This means a lot to me." The judge smiles and hands me a blue ribbon. I look out over the crowd as I walk back down, but there's still no sign of Dylan. My parents and Liam are waiting at the bottom of the stairs, and Mom hugs me tight before I'm barely on the ground again.

"We're so proud of you, honey," she says.

"Thanks, Mom." Dad tousles my hair and I look up to his beaming face. "Thanks, Dad."

"Are you ready to go?" he asks.

"You guys can go home without me. I still have to clean up and stuff," I tell them.

They look at each other cautiously. Dad nods at her and Mom says, "Okay, hun. We'll see you at home. We're so proud of you."

"Thanks, Mom," I say as they leave.

When they're gone, I turn to Liam. "I saw him leave a couple minutes ago," he tells me. "He stared at me the whole time he walked out the door."

I exhale. "Okay, good. Thanks, Liam."

"No problem. Do you need help cleaning up?"

"No, I've got it. Thanks, though. I'll see you tomorrow."

"Okay. Bye, Parker."

I say goodbye and head over to my station. As I am cleaning

up at my table, the announcer thanks all the participants and supporters. I take down my drawing, roll it up, and put it into its holder as Mr. Benjamin walks over to me. "Congratulations, Parker. Second place is very good!" he says.

"Oh, thank you, Mr. Benjamin," I say.

He looks at me for a second with what I perceive to be apprehension, and he asks, "Is everything okay, Parker? You look a little pale."

"Yeah, just surprised." It's not the whole truth, but I can't just *tell* him the truth.

"Of course. Do you have a ride home?"

"Yeah, I have my bike."

"Okay. Well I'll see you on Monday, then. Congratulations again."

I thank him again before he walks away, and then I then grab the container and walk out the door. It's pretty dark outside for a spring night, so I quickly walk over to the bike rack and kneel down to unlock my bike.

Without a sound to warn me, a hand covers my mouth, and I'm rapidly pulled away and dragged over to the side of the school. I don't even have enough time to think before my eyes focus and I see Dylan's fist coming at me and punching me in the face. He hits me square in the jaw, and I taste blood almost immediately as it shoots from my mouth. My arms are held tight behind me, so I can't defend myself, and after a few more blows to my face, my head feels so heavy I can barely lift it or see him in front of me. I try to kick him, but he punches me in the stomach, and then I'm dropped to my knees by whoever was holding me up.

This is it, I think. *This is the end. This is how it all ends. Dylan waited until I was alone. He waited until it was dark. He probably saw Liam leave without me. He wanted me at my most vulnerable. He never would have tried this if Liam had been here.*

Liam.

Another punch to my face and a kick to my stomach send

me crashing to the ground. I taste more blood in my mouth. It mixes with salty tears as I lie on my side with my face in the grass. I feel it gush out and run all down my jaw.

He's going to kill me.

"I think he gets the point, Dylan," I hear someone say behind me.

He kicks me a few final times in my stomach and shins. The last thing I hear is someone repeating Dylan's name, and after that, everything's black.

Ten

D ylan opened his front door to Liam and me standing on his front steps. "Hey, guys," he said as he welcomed us in. The smell of smoke wafted through the house and strangled my throat as it pushed to get outside into the crisp fall air. I started to cough a little. Liam didn't cough and I thought that he must be used to this. "Sorry, my mom has some friends over," Dylan said.

"That's okay," I managed to say while trying to clear my lungs of second-hand smoke.

We followed him into his living room, where Mrs. Baker and three other people were sitting. Later on, Dylan told us one of the guys was his mom's current boyfriend. I was trying to figure out how they could breathe in there, when his mom said, "Hi, boys. We'll be out of your way once the pizza gets here. You can join us if you want."

I thought she must have meant watching TV and not going out, but I wasn't certain. "No thanks, Mom; we're just gonna hang out in the basement," Dylan told her.

"Okay. Have fun," she said as we walked out of the room.

"You can put your stuff in my room. I'll meet you downstairs," Dylan said by the basement door.

Liam and I walked upstairs to Dylan's room and dropped

off our stuff near his bed. I looked around his room for the first time. There were posters of hockey teams and trophies all over the walls. "You'll get used to the smoke," Liam said.

"Really?" I asked.

"Eventually. Other than that, Dylan's mom is really nice."

"She seems nice," I said as we left his room.

His basement was like nothing I'd ever seen before. You could walk out into the backyard through a set of doors and there were hardwood floors and dark wood panelling on the walls. It had a huge theatre system, a pool table, and a bar, where he was standing, mixing drinks. "Don't worry, they're virgins," he said with a sly smirk as he handed me a blue drink in a tall glass. "For now." Liam smiled at him with a devious grin, as I took a sip. It just tasted like juice. "We'll wait 'til my mom leaves," Dylan added.

After he'd handed Liam a purple drink in another tall glass, we watched the first period of the hockey game before the pizza arrived. Then his mom and her friends left. After we had watched the last two periods, overtime, and a shootout, Dylan got up and surveyed a wall of movies. He put one in and walked over to the bar, where he started taking out bottles of alcohol from a cabinet and setting them on the counter.

"Do you want something, Parker?" he asked me as I surveyed the bottles from the couch.

"Um ... no," I said. "I'm okay right now."

The only time I'd ever had alcohol had been the month before, on Thanksgiving, when Mom had let me have a sip of wine. She'd regretted it afterwards. She was sure social services were going to come and take me away. Dad told her not to overreact. I was eleven then, and I was only twelve at this moment.

"Okay. Do you want your usual, Liam?" he asked. I looked over at Liam. Apparently, I was the only twelve-year-old in the room.

"No, thanks. Maybe later," he said. I wondered why he'd said no.

Dylan made his drink and then sat down to watch the movie. It turned out to be rated 18A, and it was one that my parents would never have let me see. I wasn't interested in it the same way that Dylan had been, but I pretended that I was. He didn't need to know that I was secretly watching the guys while he was making comments about the girls. After the movie, and a couple hours of video games and Dylan drinking, we went to his room and got ready for bed. He fell asleep pretty fast. Liam and I lay on the floor in our sleeping bags and talked.

"When is his mom getting home?" I asked.

"She probably won't be home 'til tomorrow morning," he said.

I looked over at him. He was staring at the ceiling. "What do you mean?" I asked.

"That's just how it is," he explained, as if he'd had to explain it more than once. "When she goes out, she usually stays out the whole night."

I sat up and looked at Dylan's alarm clock. "But it's four in the morning."

"Yeah, but that's just how it is. You can't change it." I lay back down and stared at the ceiling. This seemed so strange. Liam suddenly turned towards me. "Don't tell your parents, okay? They'd just freak out. We've done this a million times, and we've always been fine."

"Do your parents know?"

"No."

We didn't say anything after that. I just stared at the ceiling and thought about how strange and new that whole experience had been.

———————

Drip ... drip ... drip.
Squeak ... squeak.
Whoosh.

I wake up. My eyes are still closed, but I know those sounds. I'm in a hospital. I think about my surroundings for a moment before opening my eyes.

Beside me, there will be medical equipment with one of those clear plastic bags that collects or releases liquid into your system.

Outside the room, there will be nurses in perfectly white sneakers. They're the kind of sneakers your grandma wears, but the nurses will swear they're not the same. They're coming and going with charts for all the patients and smiles on their faces if they're nice.

In other rooms, sliding glass doors will be opening and closing. Families will be waiting with their loved ones as they wait to hear from the doctor (who has finally arrived) whether the results are good or bad.

When I open my eyes, I'll be in a white room with blinding white lights. In a bed with white sheets. With a window leading out into a dark world.

My head is pounding, and everything hurts everywhere. I slowly and painfully open my eyes to see my parents standing at the end of the bed. They don't know I'm awake yet.

"Why did I let him go on his own? We should have waited for him. It was so late!" Mom hysterically turns in small circles and runs her hands through her hair.

I close my eyes again, exhausted. I try thinking about what happened, but my mind is blurry. When I open them again, Dad is hugging her. He looks scared—like, really scared. Not just the kind of scared he sets aside when watching his team trailing four points behind at a home game in the third period. "It's okay. He's going to be fine," he assures her and kisses the top of her head.

I attempt to speak, not knowing what will happen when I do. "Mom?"

They practically bolt over to me. "Parker ... baby," Mom says, quickly taking my hand in hers. "We're so sorry." She's crying now.

"Dad?"

"Hey, Park." He looks exhausted, but he tries to smile, for my sake, I think.

"What happened? How did I get here?" I ask them.

He takes in a deep breath and looks at me as if he doesn't want to believe what he's about to say. "When you didn't come home from the school last night, we called the police and went out looking for you," he says. "They found you lying beside the school, unconscious and …" He has a hard time recalling the event, and Mom squeezes my hand tighter. It hurts, but I let her. Dad continues, "Do you remember what happened?"

I think for a minute, trying to put the pieces together, and then nod at him, but suddenly I'm not able to speak.

"Parker … Please don't tell me it was Dylan again," he says with deep despair in his eyes.

I don't want to tell him it was. If I do, he'll do something drastic and make everything a big deal. But even if I don't, I already know he knows it was him. I close my eyes as tears slip down my face, and he wipes them away. "It was," I say quietly, reluctantly.

Anger fills his eyes as he walks away from me and over to the door. "That's it!" he screams. Nurses on the other side of the glass door look up from their work. "I've had it with this kid! I'm going to press charges. And we're taking you out of that school!"

"Dad, please," I struggle to sit up and plead with him.

"No. He's taken this too far. Just two days ago we talked to him, and now he does this! We should have stopped this a long time ago."

"Mark, we can talk about this later," Mom says.

He takes a breath. "You're right. I'm sorry." He shakes his head and looks at me before looking towards the door. "I'll be right back," he says.

I watch him walk out of the room and then look over at Mom. I'm terrified. "Is Dad really going to?" I ask her. "It'll only make things worse."

"I'm sorry, baby, but this isn't your decision anymore."

"But he's going to kill me, Mom. He already tried."

"Baby, please, don't talk like that. We're trying to avoid you getting hurt."

"But it'll just make him even angrier at me."

She doesn't say anything more. She just brushes the hair away from my face.

The next day Liam comes to visit me. He says he wanted to come sooner, but my parents told him I needed to rest. He walks over to the bed with one hand behind his back as I sit up. "Hey," he says softly.

"Hey."

"How are you feeling?"

"I hurt everywhere."

He stares at me for a while and then says, "How bad is it?"

"I have a bruised kidney and black eye. The rest of me is just bruised all over."

He looks down at the floor with guilt-ridden eyes. "I should have stayed with you. I should have made sure he had actually left. I'm so sorry."

"This isn't your fault, Liam."

"I feel like it is."

"It isn't. He would have done it eventually."

He looks at me again and then holds up orange flowers he'd been hiding. "Oh, these are from my mom," he says, putting them on the table.

"Tell her I say thank you."

He smiles at me. "I will. So, what did your parents say?"

"They're pressing charges."

"Man, that's intense."

"Just another day in my crazy life," I say with a shrug, demoting the level of the situation from extreme to average.

He sits on the bed with me. "So when are you getting out of here?"

"The doctors say it could be up to a week. They say I'm traumatized, so I should stay in a safe place." I take a deep breath as he stares at me, and finally I work up the courage to ask, "Was he at school?"

"Yeah."

"Did he say anything?"

"He stared at me the whole day, but nothing else."

I nod. "Good."

He looks away at the wall for a moment, and I see his eyes turn up as he smiles. I wonder what he's thinking about until he turns back to me and says, "Do you know the moment I knew we'd always be best friends?" I shake my head, and his smile grows. "It was the day I slammed the door after leaving my house for school," he laughs. "I think I scared you."

"You were so upset." I laugh too.

"Because my mom said I couldn't go to that concert. And you told me your parents weren't letting you go, either. I hated being twelve."

"That's when you knew?" I ask.

He nods. "I'd never had a friend who liked the exact same music I liked. Dylan always despised anything good I ever tried to get him to listen to. I knew I couldn't let you get away after that," he smiles. "When the night of the concert finally came, we opened the windows in my room and blasted their albums for hours for the neighbourhood to hear."

"It was almost like we were there," I smile, remembering that unforgettable moment we'd shared in his bedroom. When we were completely alone for the first time, as our parents were out and were trusting us in his house like adults.

He pulls out a deck of cards from his back pocket and smiles. "Wanna play Go Fish?"

"Okay."

———————

"I told you that wasn't him," Liam said to me as we walked into my house, laughing, after school on a Friday afternoon.

I smiled at him. "Fine. I guess you're right."

"Well, of course I am," he said jokingly as we dropped our bags by the stairs and walked towards the kitchen.

I heard Mom call my name, and we made our way over to the laundry room instead. "Yeah?" I said standing in the doorway.

"I need that hoodie," she said, gesturing towards the one I was wearing as she continued putting clothes in the washing machine.

"Why do you need it?" I asked.

"Because it has to be washed, Parker." The tone of her voice let me know I'd better just do as she said and not ask questions.

I thought about this quickly. I couldn't take it off. If I did, she'd see the cuts I'd made on my wrist. "I'll give it to you later," I said, turning back around.

"No, I need it now, Parker," she said.

"Why?" I asked, facing her again.

She shot me a fatigued look. "I'm going out soon, and I'm already ten minutes late. If it doesn't go in now—"

"Just do it later," I said, cutting her off.

She shot me another look, though this one showed some shock at the way I'd talked to her. "Parker," she said sternly.

"I'm sorry."

"Can I please have it now?" she asked.

I was standing just outside the doorway. Liam was sitting on the stairs, pretending to look at something on the ceiling. "No," I said.

"Parker, seriously," she said, irritated. "What's going on with you?" I felt so awful to do this to her, but I couldn't take it off. She finished putting detergent into the machine and then walked over to me, leaving the machine door open. "Fine. If you won't, I will," she said, as she reached for the zipper and started pulling it down. *This can't happen*, I thought. I quickly turned around and bolted past Liam and up the stairs to my room. "Parker!" I heard her call after me.

I quickly unzipped the hoodie the rest of the way and threw

it on the floor before I even thought to close my bedroom door. I grabbed a new one from my drawer and put it on.

Liam appeared in the doorway and gave me a warning look that said I'd better be careful. No sooner had he sat on my bed than Mom walked into the room.

"Parker," she said once again as I picked the hoodie off the floor and held it out to her. She stared at me, frustrated, but more confused, before taking the offering. "Thank you," she said, eyeing me a little curiously. She looked over at Liam on the bed and then back to me. "I'm going out now. I'll be home later tonight." She stepped forward and kissed me on the head, took one last look at Liam and me, and left the room, closing the door behind her.

I exhaled and looked over at Liam. He was just staring at me, with disappointment written all over his face. "What?" I asked him.

He didn't say anything. He just kept staring at me.

"You don't understand," I told him.

Nothing.

"What would you do!" I yelled at him, frustrated at myself for being in this mess.

He put his head down. I felt awful about how sad I was making him. The worst part of all, though, was that he thought I had only cut myself once. He didn't know that I'd kept doing it. I looked around the room, trying to find an answer, but I couldn't find one.

Eleven

I wake up alone in the hospital around six in the morning a couple days later and lie completely still while listening to the liquid dripping, the shoes squeaking on tiled floors, and the doors sliding open and closed. It smells like a hospital. It makes me sick. Everything seems too familiar. I've been in this movie once before. Two years ago. I was fourteen.

It was still early when both Mom and Dad had left for work. I wouldn't be meeting Liam in front of his gate for another fifteen minutes. I wouldn't be meeting him again ever.

As soon as I heard the front door lock, I began walking slowly to my parents' bathroom. Their bed was made, but some clothes were dumped in a pile beside the hamper. I picked them up and placed them inside before putting the top back on the wicker basket. In the bathroom, I opened the medicine cabinet. I'd been searching through the house for a while, looking for something I could take. Something to numb the pain. Anything would do. Mom still kept prescription medication I'd had to take one time.

I grabbed it and took it back to my room. I popped off the top. It went flying and I assume it hit the floor. I was too busy shovelling the pills down my throat to notice. I never counted how many there were. I just hoped that however many were in there would do the trick. I was—am—pretty small, after all, so I didn't think I would need too many.

I gagged as I forced myself to swallow every single one with spit and water. When I managed to gulp down the last one, I tossed the blue bottle onto the carpet next to the lid. I noticed one more pill sitting on the floor next to the white cap. It almost blended into the beige carpet, but instead it stared right up at me. I thought about picking it up. I was about to. But I just couldn't stand the thought of having to gag one more dry, chalky pill down my sore throat. So I didn't. I left the final one on the floor.

I wasn't thinking anymore. About anything. I wasn't thinking about the time on the clock or my parents on their way to work. I didn't worry that maybe one of them would come back for something they forgot.

I didn't think about Liam getting ready just a handful of front doors away from me. I didn't think about him waiting outside his gate for me. I didn't think about him as he began wondering where I was. I didn't think about going to school, because I knew I never had to go again.

I didn't think about Dylan. Not about all the awful, derogatory names he'd ever called me. Not about his fists aimed at my face. Not about crashing or bleeding or crying.

I was done.

My mind was empty.

My mind was made up.

And my mind was beginning to fade away from me.

After a while, I started to feel something kick in. My body was beginning to feel lighter. Distant. I knew it was time to move this along. I opened my bottom dresser drawer and took out the razor. I'd found another one in the garage after Liam had taken my other one away.

My last thought, as I sat on the floor across from the empty pill bottle and prepared to gouge into my wrists, was of Liam. The boy I loved who would never love me back. Would never share the same feelings or thoughts I had for him. Liam Eriksson had never been the reason I decided to kill myself. He was what kept me living for so long. He was wonderful. My best friend. My protector. But I was just done with everything else. As I touched metal to skin, I thought about his interesting smile, and the freckles on his beautiful face, and his bright eyes that I'd looked into for the first time on my first day of school ...

I vaguely remember hearing Mom screaming and crying. I do remember being carried by someone and how freezing cold I was and the agonizing pain I felt at the bottom of my arms. I was in this daze, but I remember hearing sirens and seeing hazy visions of people moving around me. People were talking and other people were poking sharp objects into my arms. I think I struggled for a while, not wanting their strange devices near me, but after a while I stopped fighting, and then I floated away. I don't remember anything else until I woke up.

Mom was sitting on the hospital bed holding my hand when I opened my eyes. The first thing I felt was the pain in my wrists, then the pain in my stomach and acidic feeling stinging the back of my throat, which caused me to choke.

Dad was pacing back and forth by the window. I wondered what he was looking at and what time it was. What day was it? Were the leaves still beginning to bloom on the trees? How long had I slept for? And why wasn't I dead?

I realized then that my plan hadn't worked. I was still here. Alive. Something had gone wrong. I wondered how much trouble I was in and was afraid to find out. What a messed-up kid they had ended up with. They were gonna be so mad, I just knew it.

I looked down in the direction of the pain and saw bandages wrapped around both of my wrists. Mom noticed me staring at them and looked up at me with distraught eyes I knew I'd never be able to get out of my mind. "Baby ..." she said with an airy voice. Her face was pale, and her eyes were bloodshot and teary.

Dad walked over and sat on the other side of the bed. His face matched hers. Tired and lost. "Hey, Parker," he said.

I couldn't speak. I was trying to choke back tears and breathe at the same time. My eyes watered as Mom rubbed my right hand. It hurt, and I had to pull it back a bit, which hurt even more as I attempted to use muscle and tissue I had destroyed. She got the hint and stopped. I didn't want her to, though. I wanted the reminder that she was there. I took a deep breath as the weight of the world returned to me.

When I tried to speak, I realized just how badly my stomach and throat hurt. Everything was sore, and this awful taste wouldn't leave the back of my mouth. I could barely make the words and tried to clear my throat first. "I'm sorry," I managed to cough up as my voice cracked and tears ran down my face.

This made Mom cry, and that made me cry more. I saw tears in Dad's eyes, but I knew he was trying to be strong for all three of us. He wiped away the tears on my cheeks and looked at me. "We were so scared," he said. "You lost a lot of blood." Mom sniffled, and I carefully entwined my fingers between hers, even though it hurt. "Why would you do this, Parker?" His voice was sterner now, but he still carried sadness.

I couldn't look him in the eyes. "I don't know," I said sheepishly.

He wasn't buying my innocent act. "Yes you do. People don't just do this kind of thing, Parker." I chose not to say anything to that. As much as he wanted to, I didn't want to dredge up the past right then and there. "If I hadn't been so close to the house yesterday morning when Liam called me, I might not have gotten to you in time."

I looked up at him. Had Liam really found me? Had I really put him through that again?

"Liam?" I asked softly.

"He found you in your bedroom. Apparently for the second time," Dad said eyeing me. I couldn't stand to face him, so I just looked down at the white sheets. "He said you were lying on the floor and your arms and hands were covered in blood," he told me and sighed. "There was an empty bottle of your old pain medication lying on the floor beside you. They had to pump your stomach to get everything out."

I started crying again. I'd forgotten about the pills I'd taken. All those pills. I had wanted to take something to relieve the pain I was about to feel, and since they kept any alcohol locked up good, I'd known the medication in their medicine cabinet was the only choice. There weren't many pills left, but I had taken all of them. Except for that one that fell on the floor. "I'm sorry," I said again.

"We know you're sorry, Parker. We want to know why you would do this," he said.

I took a deep breath, preparing to tell them exactly how I felt. "Because they make my life hell, Dad!" I was angry then. "I couldn't take it. The thought of going to school just so I can be laughed at and pushed around makes me sick!"

"You know you can always talk to us about anything, though," Mom said sweetly.

I looked at her. She was so destroyed. She couldn't understand why her son would do this to himself, and she hated that there was nothing she could do to stop it. But that was the point, right? This was what I wanted to do. I just didn't want to wake up. "I know. But sometimes talking doesn't feel like enough," I said.

"Cutting yourself should never be the 'enough' you need to feel," Dad said.

"Then what am I supposed to do?"

They exchanged looks between one another and it made me nervous. "We've arranged for you to see a psychologist," Dad said. I opened my mouth to object, but they cut me off. The last thing I wanted was to talk to a stranger about my problems. And I'd just acquired one more issue to add to the top of the pile. Didn't sound like a fun Wednesday evening to me. "You'll see him twice a week, for six weeks, and then we'll go from there," he explained. "It's either that or you stay here at the hospital. You'd be transferred to the psychiatric ward for an undetermined amount of time and see a therapist there."

He said this as seriously as I've ever heard him. It almost didn't even sound like him.

"So, either way, I have to talk to someone?" I asked, repulsed by the idea. "What if I don't want to?"

"You're in the Crisis Stabilization Unit, Parker," he said. "For attempted suicide."

It took a second for those words to sink in.

Attempted suicide.

That was the bottom.

I later learned that the Crisis Stabilization Unit was the emergency room for dealing with suicidal and violent people. It was hard to imagine that I was there. I guess there was an option to leave me there or to transfer me to the juvenile ward—in other words, the psychiatric ward. They decided to let me go home and recommended that I get professional help. I guess after spending a few nights in the hospital, they thought I wasn't a threat to myself anymore, so I didn't have to be a prisoner much longer.

I knew there was no point in arguing. The decision was made, and I had no choice but to see the psychologist. My parents were silent for a while as they tried to put together the pieces that had led to this moment. Mom's hand never left mine.

"Are you mad at me?" I finally asked, terrified of the answer.

"We're mad that you didn't come to talk to us first. And we're mad by how scared you made us. But we're so glad that you're okay," Mom said.

I had the feeling that they had probably been coached by the nurses beforehand on what to say. I couldn't imagine parents not being mad after finding their child bleeding on their bedroom floor.

I tried to make the effort to smile, but it didn't go through.

"Liam's here," Dad said after a while. "He's been pretending to read magazines in the waiting room for three hours. Do you want to see him?" I looked up a little and nodded. "Okay," he said before patting me on the leg. Mom let go of my hand and kissed my forehead. Then they both left the room, and I stared at the speckled ceiling.

I began seriously thinking about what I had done and about how scared it had made them. I felt the bandages on my wrist as the door opened and Liam walked in.

He looked terrible, as if he hadn't slept in days. I probably looked worse. He slowly walked over and stood by the side of the bed. I sat up and matched his gaze. I didn't know what to say to him.

"You promised," he said. His voice was higher than normal, and it shook almost uncontrollably.

"I know. I'm sorry," I told him. I hated myself for breaking that promise.

His face. His scared and bloodshot eyes that looked at the ground and then at me, his pale skin where colour should be, his chapped lips that he kept chewing on. It made me grateful to have the chance to see him again. "You really scared me," he said. I could feel the tremble in his voice as he managed to choke out those five syllables without a single tear shed from his glistening eyes. He held his hands behind his back the whole time, twisting them together. Maybe he was keeping himself from strangling me for scaring him so badly.

"I'm sorry," I repeated quietly. If I said any more I'd start crying.

"No, screw this," he said without yelling. "You promised me, Parker Knight. You promised me." I attempted to speak, but he cut me off. "And you didn't even say goodbye!" He yelled that one and I felt his agony in every thread of my being. "Not even a note?"

He look a deep breath and sat on the bed with me, both of us staring at the stark white sheets. Suddenly he was so overwhelmed and started bawling his eyes out. I'd never seen him cry before, let alone to this degree. He covered his face with one hand, while the other clutched the sheet beside my leg. He did this for a while as he let tears fall, and I just stared at him. When he took his hand away, some colour had been restored to his cheeks. He wiped his face, even though he wasn't finished crying, and said, "When I saw you lying on your floor …" He paused to take a gasp of air and then continued, "I thought you were dead."

That started me up crying, too. Imagining him walking in on my lifeless body.

"I called your dad and 911, and they took you to the hospital." His shaky voice paused for another second. "I honestly thought you were going to die. I saw the bottle on the floor and all the blood and completely freaked out." After he said this, we became quiet for a while. We were both picturing the scene in our heads. Then he said, "I don't know what I'd do without you. I really don't. You're my best friend."

"You're my best friend too," I told him.

"You can't do this anymore, Parker. I won't let you destroy your life because of him. He's not worth it. Don't give him the satisfaction of winning. Please."

I couldn't make any words, so I just nodded. As hard as it was, I knew he was right. Not entirely at that moment, but over time, I came to realize it more. He leaned forward and hugged me tightly, as if he were afraid I was going to drift away. His hands clutched at my back and pulled me closer to him. It hurt too much to lift my arms, so I just nestled my head on his shoulder with my chin tucked into his collarbone and cried. He placed his head gently on my shoulder, and with every breath he took that weighed down and lifted off me, I let myself begin to trust anything he said.

Don't give him the satisfaction of winning. I repeated it over and over in my head.

I still think about those words. Every day, actually. I couldn't see it very well back then, but Liam was right. Letting Dylan win would be too easy. Sure, the fight would be over, but he didn't deserve to win. He *doesn't* deserve to win.

"It'll be over soon. I promise," he told me. "Just hold on. I'll be here the whole time."

I nestled in closer as he held me tighter. I didn't want to let go of his warm body and his sweet smell and his soft hair on my face, so I just closed my eyes.

———————

A nurse walks into the room and smiles at me. "Good morning, Parker," she says sweetly. "You're up pretty early."

"I couldn't sleep," I tell her.

She looks at charts and monitors beside my bed. "I don't blame you. With all these machines and unfamiliar hospital noises, it's hard for some people to fall asleep."

"It's not that."

"Oh, is something else wrong that I can fix for you?"

"I don't think so." She looks at me with caring eyes and waits for me to continue. "I'm afraid to go back to school when I go home."

"Oh, I see. Because of the kid who did this to you?"

I nod.

She sits down on the bed with me. "I know I'm just an old person who doesn't understand," she says, and it makes me smile because she's not old at all. "But I do know something about bullies." She leans in closer as if she's telling me a secret, and I lean in, too. "They're scared," she says. "They put down others to make themselves feel better because they're insecure. They make fun of the things they don't understand."

"I don't think he's scared," I tell her.

"You'd be surprised," she says. "When I was your age, there were a bunch of girls who would tease me because I was smart. They liked to trip me in the halls so I would drop my books, and they called me names."

"How did you deal with that?"

"Well, I decided I had two options. I could try to be friends with them, or I could ignore them, stick up for myself, and put a stop to it."

"What did you do?"

"I tried to be friends with them at first. I said hi to them in the hall. I even offered to help them with their homework, but that didn't work, and it won't always work. So I ignored them. I pretended like they weren't there."

"And they stopped?"

"No, they didn't stop."

"Oh."

"Unfortunately, I had to live through it for the rest of high school, but once I graduated, I never had to see them again. I went to college and made something out of myself, out of the qualities they teased me for."

"But what happens when it just gets too hard?"

"You hold on tighter. Life is hard on everybody, but it won't always be this hard. Just hold on. The good part is yet to come."

"Okay," I say softly. It's all I can say. She gets up and touches my hand before walking over to the door. "Thank you," I say when she opens it.

She turns around and smiles before walking out.

It seems that everyone over the years has been telling me the same thing. Maybe that really does means something. I stare at the hospital ceiling, thinking and remembering. Everything externally hurts. Everything internally hurts. But I think internally hurts more.

———————

I was sitting on my bedroom floor, crying. I'd run home so fast from Grade 8 that day. Liam was home sick, so I had to try even harder not to be seen by Dylan. I'd managed to hide from him the whole day. My heart had been racing when I walked out of school. I'd thought I had actually escaped the hate. But I'd been wrong.

I heard him from behind me. "Hey, Parker," he said. I could hear the wickedness in his voice, like a snake in a child's cartoon.

I looked over my shoulder to see him, Avery, and Ethan walking towards me. It felt as if the sky became dark, and the whole world seemed to cave in on me. Walking home from school, I always had Liam with me. Always.

"Where's your boyfriend, Parker?" he asked in the same voice.

I looked forward again and started running as fast as I could. I could hear their footsteps pick up behind me, and with every step I took, I prayed they wouldn't catch me. I needed to be faster than them. *Please.*

I turned the corner that led into my neighbourhood. The puddle beneath me splashed hard as I landed on it. I could hear the same puddles splashing again and again and again under the pressure of hatred as the three of them trailed behind me. I tried to run faster, but it was a chilly day, and the cold wind made it hard to breathe. I couldn't let myself give out, though. It would be over soon. Just as soon as I got to my house.

I could hear them yelling at me from a distance. If I hadn't gotten a head start, I never would have been this far from them. *Just keep running,* I told myself. *Don't stop now. Don't stop.*

I turned another corner and raced the final distance down the block and up my driveway, as I struggled to find the key in my front pocket. I didn't look back to see where they were. I didn't have enough time or courage. I jammed the key into the deadbolt and unlocked the door. When the door was locked again, I was safe. I threw my bag on the floor and ran upstairs. In my room, I fell onto my knees, screaming and crying as loudly as I could with my fists wrapped tightly around my hair.

I pulled up my sleeves and then pulled open the bottom dresser drawer and took it out. Holding it in my right hand, I sat on the floor and dragged it across my left arm. I didn't do it too hard. Just scratches. But it was enough to make me feel something. I needed to take my mind off Dylan.

I heard a knock on my door and stopped in fear, quickly hiding the razor beneath me and pulling my sleeves down. I looked up as my dad walked in. He looked terrified, and within seconds he was kneeling in front of me, with his hands on my shoulders. "Parker," he said. It made me tremble and cry. He continued, "Didn't you hear me calling you?"

I thought about the last few moments and wondered how long they had lasted. Minutes? Seconds? I shook my head.

"What happened?" he asked me while moving the hair off my face.

I was choking back tears that made my throat hurt, and I couldn't say anything. When he figured out I wasn't going to talk, he let out a sigh, sat down, and wrapped his arms around me. He held me while my head rested against his chest, and I bawled exhaustedly.

I'd managed not to get caught that day, and there were other times, too. I never told Liam how many there were. He thought that because he'd taken the razor away from me the first time, I couldn't do it anymore. But of course, I just found another one. I was too ashamed to admit it to him, or even myself, so I just let it keep happening.

The fluorescent lighting gives me a headache, so I close my eyes.

Twelve

In the bathroom mirror at home, I check out my bruised stomach. Dad did what he said he was going to do and filed an assault charge against Dylan, with a temporary restraining order. It wasn't hard to find evidence, what with all the bruises, cuts, and bleeding found on my body. Plus we have a history that the school staff, parents, psychologist, and hospital employees are well aware of.

By the way, this is bad for me. You might think it's good, because now Dylan is expected to stay away from me. But this is Dylan. Is he really going to listen to rules, even if they *are* ordered by the city police? All of this is just making a bad situation even more horrible, because I don't want him to have one more thing against me, and I really don't want him to kill me. I just want to forget it ever happened. But now this is going to make him even angrier at me. Maybe it will even be on his permanent record.

It would be an understatement to say that Dad is less than pleased. I can always tell when he's really mad about something when I hear him working in the garage for hours with the table saw. He says it's his way of dealing with stuff, and by the end of it all, Mom always ends up with something nice, like a cool flowerpot or a clock. This time it's a bench for the backyard. I can tell Mom is angry too, but she shows it in a more delicate way, and it's more like sympathy than rage. She's spent so much time watching TV with me that I've actually got her quoting my favourite shows—even the ones she still says are too morbid and gory for her. Too much blood, I suppose.

*   *   *

"What about this guy?" Liam asks, pointing to a model posing in an advertisement for a clothing company in a magazine. He picked it up for me as a joke. Because he knows I'm *really* into knowing what celebrities are doing every waking moment.

"He's too preppy," I shrug. "But his eyes are nice."

We're sitting on my bedroom floor with the magazine while working on my late homework. Every few minutes he'll lean forward and point at something on my page. I get to smell his body wash every time he does. I think it's mango and peach. "You forgot to do this or that," he'll say to me and then smile and go back to flipping through the glossy pages.

"Okay," he says, "What about this guy?"

I look up from English homework at the actor beside his finger. The one they've spotted walking down the street after leaving the gym. As if that deserves to be world news. "He's pretty cute," I say, remembering a movie he was in that we saw last summer. Liam smiles and is about to turn the page, but I stop it and ask, "What about her?" I point to the actress on the next page, walking her dog through a park.

He shrugs his shoulders. "She's wearing heels while walking her dog. That seems kinda high maintenance."

We never talk about girls. Or guys. I guess I was a little curious to see what he would say. "So, what do you like, tomboys?" I ask.

He shrugs again. "I guess." Then he points to my paper again and explains what I've done wrong. "Here, let me do it," he says as he takes the pencil from my hand to start scribbling down the right answer.

I let the feeling of his perfect fingers touching my hand linger for a while before I let it slide off.

*   *   *

The hospital let me go home about a week ago. Liam came to see me every day after school. My face is healing "quite nicely" according to the doctors, and the bruises on my stomach are slowly going away. The doctors say it will be another week before I am completely back to normal.

I'm not going to school right now, and my parents thought that, with all this emotionally heavy stuff happening to me, it might be a good idea to do something to clear my head during the day. So I've been volunteering at the SPCA a couple times a week. I didn't know whether I'd like it, but I do, and now I can't imagine not doing it. I'm in charge of exercising and feeding the dogs, and sometimes I hang out in the cat room and play with the kittens.

There's this one dog, named Snickers, who I've bonded with. He's a three-year-old white lab who was a stray. They found him just a couple weeks ago in a back alley. He was skinny and sick, but he had surprising energy and optimism.

"Your mom's here, Parker!" Linda, the administrator, yells out to me from the door.

"Okay, I'll be right there!" I shout from the far end of the field where I am playing with the dogs along with the other volunteers. I scratch Snickers behind the ear and tell him I'll be back in three days to see him. Then I say goodbye to the others and run across the field and into the building. Mom is reading a pamphlet by the front desk when I get there.

"Hey, Mom."

"Hi, hun. How are your animals?"

I laugh. She has this way of being funny that she doesn't even realize she has. "They're good."

"Good. Are you ready to go?"

"Yeah," I say before we walk out into the warm evening.

These weeks have become bittersweet. I love that I can stay home every day and draw and volunteer with the animals and I don't want it to end. But I know that I have to go back to school someday, and when I do, he'll be waiting for me.

I haven't worked on my painting since before spring break, so this evening I finish a little more detail on the birds. The sky isn't exactly the same as that day, but I have a pretty good memory of it pictured in my mind. It's almost finished. Mom will be happy to take it to work with her soon.

Later on, I'm lying in bed, reading, when I hear my parents talking downstairs through my open bedroom door. I listen from bed for a while, but once I hear Dad say my name, I put my book down, get out of bed, and crawl across my bedroom floor. With my head sticking out of the door I can hear better. The hall light is off, but the lights downstairs are on. I don't see them, so they must be in the living room.

"I picked these up today," I hear Dad say.

"Mark, do you really think sending him to a different school is necessary?" Mom asks him.

I can't believe it. They actually want to send me to a different school? I'd thought Dad was just yelling things out back at the hospital because he was angry. I didn't think they were going to go through with it. They've already involved the police in my life. Why do they have to do this too? I can't be a new kid all over again. It was too hard the first time. Even if the kids at school don't talk to me, they at least *know* about me.

"What other choice do we have?" he asks.

"I don't know. I feel terrible. What parents would let this happen to their child?" Mom says.

It's silent all of a sudden. I hold my breath and try to listen more closely, but I can't hear anything. I push the door open a little more and slide out of my room into the hall, careful not to hit any walls. Then I creep to the top of the stairs and lie there listening.

"Maybe we can home-school him for the rest of the year," Mom suggests.

"But he'll still go back to school in the fall, and Dylan will be there."

"Maybe it will all blow over by then."

"Kids like Dylan don't just forget their victims because they're not there."

I don't like being a victim.

"Well, I just don't see any good choice. He's not going to want to leave Liam. He's his best friend. We can't do that to him."

"I know. You're right. So, what are we going to do?" he asks.

Suddenly I start feeling scratchiness at the back of my throat. I try to swallow to make it go away, but it won't. Soon my eyes became watery and I try to clear my throat quietly. It's too powerful though, and I start coughing. It's not even like a normal cough. It's an attack. I'm coughing so loudly and out of control that I don't even hear them walk over to the bottom of the stairs and look up at me. Mom walks up and sits with me while I watch Dad walk to the kitchen through teary eyes. *So much for being subtle.*

"Are you okay, Park?" Mom asks as she rubs my back.

"Yeah," I say while sitting up and continuing to cough. Dad joins us and passes me a glass of water, which I finish without breathing through it. They look at each other and then at me as I put the glass on the floor and look back at them. "Please don't send me to a different school," I beg. They go silent. "Please," I start again. "I can't leave Liam."

"We know, darling," Mom says and brushes her hand through my hair. "We just don't want you to get hurt again."

"High school is only two more years. Please," I beg.

"Aren't you scared about going back to school?" Dad asks.

I think about this for a moment. I think about all the times I had my back turned and didn't see Dylan coming up behind me to slam me into the lockers. I think about all the terrible things he's ever said to me and all the horrific names he's ever called me. And then there are all the things that have yet to happen ...

"I am scared, but ..." I say, "but when Liam's there, I just feel a little bit better. I don't want to be all alone in a new school."

Mom leans forward and takes me in her arms as I close my eyes. This is where I really feel safe.

"I'm sorry, Park, but we have no other choice," Dad says.

I nod sadly.

"You should get some sleep now, hun," Mom says.

"So when am I going back to school?"

"We don't know yet. We'll just take it day by day for now," Dad says.

"Okay."

I hug them both before going to my room, crawling back into bed, and falling asleep.

Thirteen

"**W**hat about this one?" Dad asks Mom, looking at a pamphlet for a new school in the dining room. We've been at this for hours and I'm losing my mind.

"That one has a great sports program," Mom says. "But this school has one of the highest academic ratings in the province. What do you think, Parker?" she asks me.

My head is glued to the table. I'm attempting to escape. "I don't like sports," I tell her.

"Hm ... well, what about this one?" she says to Dad.

This isn't even about me.

"This one has nice uniforms," Dad says.

"Uniforms!" I say, sitting up rapidly. They can't possibly be serious.

"Yes, Parker, uniforms," Mom says, as if it's so obvious.

"I don't want to wear a uniform!" I protest.

"They're pretty nice, though."

"But I'll look just like everybody else!"

Mom tries persuasion as a tactic. "They say the students love the sense of unity they get from wearing them."

"But I want to be myself!"

They don't say anything while they read more of the brochures that are spread out across the whole table, and I put my head back down. *This is not happening. This is not happening.*

"Park?" Mom says.

I tilt my head just enough to look at her. "Yeah?"

"This one has a great art program."

"But I already like my art class. Why would I want to leave it?"

"Because you're not safe there. That's why," Dad chimes in.

I roll my head back down, knowing I'm not going to win this battle.

They keep talking to themselves, while I try to tune them out. New schools have new students and new teachers. New unwritten rules of where everybody sits, what's normal, and what's weird. And most importantly, there's no Liam in a new school.

*   *   *

On the drive to one of the possible new schools, I stare out the window at the tall trees along the brick fence. We pull up to the gate and Dad tells the intercom who we are. The whole time I'm thinking, *What kind of school has a gate?* There are cameras on the tall posts beside it, and I feel as if they're staring at me. We drive up to an old brick school that can't be younger than a thousand years old.

"Try to keep an open mind," Mom says when we get out of the car. I don't respond as the ivy climbing up the walls of the decrepit building catches my eye.

"This place looks great," Dad says eagerly while we walk up the steps. I stare over at him and notice he's actually having fun. And this is before we've even gotten inside. I roll my eyes.

The inside is panelled with dark wood and has tall ceilings. There are pictures of old guys on the walls, and it looks more like a museum than a school. A couple of students walk by carrying books and wearing the uniforms. *I cannot let this happen.*

A receptionist greets us in the office before we sit in the waiting area.

"What do you think?" Dad asks, practically beaming.

"It's kinda stuffy, don't you think?"

He opens his mouth to disagree but then changes his mind and thinks about it. "Well, maybe a little," he admits. "But it's nice."

"What about all the security?"

"It's for your protection."

"Seems strange."

"Don't judge it too soon. Just try to be neutral. Wait 'til we talk to the principal."

As soon as he says it, the principal walks out of his office. He's dressed so nicely that he looks as though he's going to an award show rather than to school. "You must be the Knights," he says, walking over and shaking my parents' hands. "I'm Mr. Callaghan, the school principal."

"It's good to meet you," Dad says.

"You as well. Parker?" he asks in my direction.

"Hi," I say, trying to be Sweden for as long as I can.

"Why don't you all come into my office?" he says as he leads us in.

It has panelling too, and walls lined with books. It reminds me of the psychologist's office, except that my familiar brown sofa is replaced by three dark chairs. I follow Dad's lead and sit in one of them, near him.

"Well, first off, welcome to West Pointe Secondary School. We're privileged you've decided to consider us," he says.

Consider us? When did we start considering schools?

I thought we were just looking.

Fine, then. I tried.

I am no longer Sweden.

"We've read great things about the school," Mom says.

"Thank you. I assure you none of them are true," he says, and they all laugh. Old people share a weird sense of humour. "Now, if you don't mind my asking, what makes you decide to

transfer just three months before the end of the school year?"
Mr. Callaghan asks.

Great, this will be fun.

My parents look at each other shifty-like, and then Dad
tells him about my history of being the prey of a bully.

"Oh, I see," Mr. Callaghan says after, sitting back in his
chair and taking it all in.

"So you can see why we're so concerned," Mom adds.

"Yes, of course. Well, you can rest assured knowing that we
have a no-bullying policy here at West Pointe."

"That sounds great," Dad says sceptically, "but I'm sure
that doesn't entirely ensure that kids will listen."

"I see your concern, but again, I can assure you that you
will have no worries here. Our students are very well mannered
and mature. They get along great with each other, and there's
a wonderful sense of unity that comes along with that."

Mom looks across Dad and smiles at me at the word *unity.*
I hate it that she loves this so much and I don't.

The rest of the meeting is more talking about the *wonderful*
school, followed by paperwork. By the time we get back to the
car, they've got more brochures and papers than they can
handle, and they're so excited. I just wish I felt the same way.
"What did you think?" Mom asks, turning to me in the car.

I shrug. "I don't know."

I can tell she feels sorry for me. "You'd still be able to see
Liam after school," she says.

"Yeah," I say sadly.

She turns back around as I watch the world go by outside
the window.

*   *   *

"It was awful," I tell Liam, hanging my head over the side
of my bed.

"It doesn't sound that bad to me," he says from across the
room.

"Seriously? Whose side are you on?"

"Yours, but ..."

"But what?" I ask, turning over. Some blood floods back to the rest of my body after being stored in my brain.

"Well, the way I see it, you've been dealing with Dylan for, like, three years, right?"

"Right ..."

"Aren't you tired of it?" I don't answer him, so he continues, "Wouldn't you rather *not* be afraid every time you go to school?" *Of course* I'd rather not be afraid, but I don't say that, so he says, "Maybe this is your chance, you know?" I nod, but I don't mean it. "Say something," he insists.

"I don't know what to say, okay!" I hadn't expected it to be that fiery, but I realized I *was* that upset.

"You don't have to be so upset about it," he says.

"Yes, I do! I do, Liam! You're not the one whose parents are trying to switch you to a new school! You're not the one who doesn't want to go! And you're not the one who *has* to go because you can't stay at the old one!"

"Okay, I'm sorry," he says, clearly hurt.

I can't stand to yell at him anymore, so I tell him I'm tired, and he leaves. I feel awful as I watch him walk out of my room.

Downstairs, my parents are looking over papers for the new school at the kitchen table. They don't hear me come in, so I just watch them for a bit. They look so happy that I'm finally getting out of there. I feel the blood in my veins boil, and I start to burn up. My rage is kept inside like a caged animal. They eventually notice my presence and turn around. But before Dad can ask me how I am, I'm already letting out a scream. I'm sure they look shocked, but my eyes are closed.

The animal is out.

"Parker, what's going on?" Mom asks when it's silent and awkward again.

"I hate it there!" I scream. "I hate everything about that stupid school! And I hate you for making me go there!"

"Parker," Dad says sternly.

I've gone too far. But I keep going. "No! This isn't fair!"

"It's the only way we can keep you safe," Mom explains.

"Yeah, you keep telling yourselves that."

"Parker, don't talk to your mother like that," Dad says.

I've never gone this far. But instead of apologizing, as I'm sure I should and I'm sure they're thinking I'm going to, I run out of the house and slam the front door.

I'm heading for the only place I can go to think when I'm out this late. The sky is already dark. The stars sparkle and surround a crescent moon. A few people are leaving the park as I find an empty swing and plant myself on it.

I don't know how long I've been here, slowly swinging no higher than a few inches—a few hours maybe—when I hear him walk along the sand and stand beside the other swing.

"Can I sit with you?" Liam asks.

I shrug. "Sure."

He sits and stares at the sky with me. "Your parents called me. They thought you might be at my house."

I like that he's here.

But I don't tell him that.

Maybe this *is* my chance. Maybe West Pointe Secondary School is my chance to start over and forget about him. Not completely. But maybe it's finally time to get over him. It certainly doesn't seem to be doing me any good knowing it'll always be one-sided.

"Are you going to say anything?" he asks.

It's not fun being in love with someone who doesn't feel the same.

"You've never run away for this long," he says. "I don't think you've ever run away at all."

"You don't know everything I do," I say defensively.

"Okay ..." he says, puzzled by my outburst. "You should go home."

I snap at him, "Maybe you should stop telling me what to do."

He turns in his swing to look at me. "You're mad at your parents, Parker. Don't take it out on me."

"Whatever."

"Man, what is your problem?"

"You wouldn't understand."

"I'm your best friend. Of course I'd understand." I keep my secrets to myself. "Fine. Have it your way. I'll let your parents know you're safe." He gets up and walks away, and I don't do anything to stop him.

He leaves the scent of himself behind. Lingering beside me, it makes the stars seem secondary in comparison.

I eventually do make it home. And my parents are waiting for me on the stairs when I do. They start with the lecture as soon as my foot is in the door. "Do you have any idea what time it is!" Dad demands.

I don't care. I head for the kitchen.

"Don't walk away from us," he says, following me.

"Why? Why does it matter what I do? Nothing matters anymore!"

"Parker, what is going on with you?" he asks.

"Nothing!" I'm not sure that one was supposed to come out that angry either.

"Parker, you can tell us anything," Mom says.

"What are you feeling?" Dad asks.

I start screaming again.

"Parker, stop screaming and use your words," he orders.

"I'm not five, Dad!"

"Prove it," he challenges me.

"I don't have words to describe how I feel!"

"Then act it out. Draw it. Do *something*."

I don't want to. "I'm going to bed," I tell them.

He grabs my arm as I walk away and forces me to look at him, but I wrestle my way out of his grasp and run upstairs to my room.

*   *   *

Liam's waiting for me at the bottom of the driveway the next morning when I get outside. The time has finally come to go back to school, at least for the time being. I don't really want to, but I've missed two weeks, and my parents don't want me falling even farther behind. They're taking the chance in sending me back, but they've asked all the teachers to keep an extra eye on me. *Because that doesn't make me feel stupid at all.*

The temporary restraining order my parents filed has expired. It was only meant for a short time, hence the term *temporary*. So I think it was mainly used as a scare tactic. I don't think anything scares Dylan, though.

I don't know what they're thinking making me go back on a Friday, though. I run around the house, grabbing the books and homework I've left lying everywhere, pull on a white T-shirt, grab a hoodie off my bed, and run out of the house. West Pointe is still processing my passport, and they don't know how long it might take. Maybe a few weeks. I hope I never have to go to that school. But I know I can't keep going to this one. I'm so stuck.

"Hey," Liam speaks softly when I meet him at the bottom of the driveway. We begin walking to school.

I mirror his soft greeting and then remember that I yelled at him yesterday. "I'm sorry," I tell him. "I freaked out. I just feel like I'm losing control, you know? My life is such a mess right now and it makes no sense. Everything I want I can't have, and everything that's "good" for me sucks."

"I get it. Maybe it'll just work itself out."

"I yelled at my parents. I never do that."

"I'm sure they understand."

I nod. I hope so. We haven't actually talked about it yet. I went straight to bed last night and slipped out quietly this morning for school. "Have I missed a lot?" I ask.

"A little. But all the teachers are gonna give you extra time to finish."

I nod, and we keep walking for a while. Then I stop. I can't go any further. I tried to be strong in front of my parents so they wouldn't transfer me, but I'm really terrified.

"I don't think I can do it, Liam," I say.

He stops and looks at me worriedly. "It's okay."

"No, it's not. You asked me before if I still think about death, and I do. I think Dylan really wants to kill me."

"Parker ..."

"He does, Liam. He's made it pretty obvious."

"He can't hurt you if teachers are around. He may be the worst person I know, but I don't think he'll kill you."

I take a deep breath. I want to believe him, but I don't.

"Are you okay now?" he asks.

"No."

We start walking to school again anyways, and then Liam says, "You won't have to defend yourself on your own."

I smile at him. That's why Liam Eriksson is my best friend.

I have a doctor's note that says I'm excused from gym, but I still have to be there, so I sit on the bench, occasionally looking up to see what everybody else is doing, but mostly just doing social studies homework.

For whatever reason, I'm so intrigued by my homework that I don't even see the plastic ball aimed straight for me. But it hits me right in the stomach and knocks the wind out of me. I fall onto my knees on the gym floor and start coughing up blood while trying to catch my breath.

From across the gym, I hear a whistle blow and Liam scream. I look up just in time to see him tackle Dylan to the floor and our gym teacher run over to break it up, but not before Liam punches Dylan in the face. Then he's picked up by Mr. Van Dorsen and restrained.

"What the hell is wrong with you! Why do you hate him so much?" Liam screams.

Dylan sits up with a bloody nose. "Did you see what he did to me?" he asks Mr. Van Dorsen. "He's crazy."

"I'm the crazy one?" Liam screams and struggles to get free.

Mr. Van Dorsen says, "I saw, Dylan. I also saw you throw the ball at Parker."

"He should have caught it."

"He's not playing, Dylan! Both of you can go to the principal's office now. I'll take Parker to the nurse."

After Mr. Van Dorsen lets go of Liam, Dylan storms out the gym doors, and Liam runs over to me. I'm still sitting on the floor, holding my internally bleeding self. "Parker. Are you okay?" Liam asks.

All I can do is moan.

Mr. Van Dorsen crouches beside me. "Parker, can you stand up?" The two of them attempt to help me stand, but my stomach hurts so bad that all I can do is moan and cough up more blood on the floor. "Okay," Mr. Van Dorsen says. "We're gonna take you to the hospital. Liam, you stay with him. I'll be right back."

Mr. Van Dorsen sits me on the bench before walking out of the room. I'm trying my hardest not to cry as Liam sits down and puts his arm around me.

Fourteen

I'm starting to feel like I live at the hospital. I'm sitting on an examination table with my parents standing close by. The doctor is looking at X-rays. When he turns around and looks at us, Dad says, "So only his kidney has had damage done to it?"

"Yes, fortunately nothing else has been impacted," the doctor tells him.

"How long will it take to heal?" Mom asks.

"Come back after a couple weeks, and we'll have another look. I'd suggest taking a week off school and avoiding any sports. Is there someone who can drop off homework for you? I wouldn't want you falling behind." I nod. "Okay. Well, we'll just finish up here with a routine check-up, and you'll be on your way."

"We'll wait for you outside, hun," Mom says.

I give them a weak smile as I watch them leave the room. The doctor rolls over on his stool and checks my heartbeat with a freezing stethoscope. "Someone must really have it out for you," he says to me.

"You don't understand. He hates me. He's been doing this for years."

He nods before saying, "There was a kid who hated me when I was young. He used to hurt me, too. Never this bad, mind you, but it certainly wasn't fun."

"What did you do?"

He checks my blood pressure.

"Well, one day, after years of taking his abuse, I just stood up to him. A bunch of us did, actually. We decided that we wouldn't take it anymore. And after that he left me alone." I don't say anything as he rolls back a bit. "Life gets better, Parker. You'll see. Just hang in there. You're free to go now. The rest of you is in good health, and you're healing quite nicely."

My parents are reading old magazines in the waiting room when I find them. They didn't mention anything about last night when they first saw me, but I know they expect it now. "I'm sorry," I say when I reach them.

"Thank you," Mom says as she hugs me.

"I should've found some other way to express how I feel," I add. They both smile. "Do I still have to go to that other school?"

"Parker," Dad says, obviously, "We're in a hospital." He puts his arm around me as we walk out of the room. It was worth a shot, at least.

What I take away from this experience is that some people do not listen to the law. Not even the threat of a restraining order could keep Dylan away from me.

Liam's sitting on our front steps when we pull into the driveway, and he walks over as soon as I get out of the car. "How are you?" he asks.

"I've been better. You?"

"Me too."

He looks over at Mom. "My mom said I can stay the rest of the day with Parker, if that's okay."

Dad and I walk into the house, and I hear them talking behind me. "Of course," she says, "that would be perfect. Parker's lucky to have a friend like you, Liam."

"He's going to be okay, right?" he asks.

"He's going to be just fine."

In my room, Liam and I are quiet. Neither of us knows what to say at first. "How bad is your bruise?" he finally asks.

"Do you want to see?"

"Yeah," he says. I stand up and lift my shirt to reveal the yellow-and-green bruise on my stomach. "Dude, that's sick," he says.

I laugh at him. "I know, right?"

Then Dad walks in and passes me a bag of ice cubes wrapped in a towel. "That *is* pretty sick, Park," he says.

Liam and I laugh at him as he messes up my hair and walks out. The ice pack feels good on my stomach as I sit back down with Liam.

"I got a week's worth of detention. Dylan did too. He should've gotten more, though," he says.

"That sucks."

"It was worth it. I bargained with Mr. Morrison to let me serve them during lunch instead of after school, so I can come over."

That doesn't surprise me at all. Liam's so charismatic and charming he could talk himself out of anything. "I'm sorry you had to get in trouble," I say.

"It's fine. It was worth it to make him bleed after everything he's done to you."

I look up and give him an appreciative smile. Even though I know it's not right to feel good over someone else's pain, I can't help it. I want Dylan to feel *something* after what he's done to me.

*   *   *

It's been a week since that day in gym class, and I'm finally not feeling so sore. Liam came over every day to bring my homework and hang out, and I'm so grateful for that. It was getting lonely being by myself all day. Most afternoons we played video games or just hung out in my room listening to music. Liam played me songs he's written on his guitar.

I heard my parents talking again one night. They said this was just one more reason to get me out of my current school and into the new one faster. They say I have one more week until I go to the new school. I'm debating whether or not to spend some more time at my current one. I want to spend some more time there with Liam, but I don't know if I can actually set foot in that place without being sent to the hospital again. I hate to admit it, but the new school does sound like a better plan, health-wise.

Tonight, while I'm tossing and turning in bed, I look over to see Liam fast asleep beside me. You'd think that after seven hours of movies and video games I'd be just as tired, but I can't fall asleep. Finally, I decide just to get up. I creep out of my room, being careful not to wake him.

Outside on the patio, there's a cool night and sweet spring air waiting for me. I lie on my back on the cold deck and look up. A sky full of stars surrounds a giant full moon. Birds flutter in a tree across the backyard and then go back to sleep.

My parents' bedroom is right above me, so I have to be careful not to wake them up. Ever since the night of the contest, they haven't slept a full night, and they haven't really let me out of their sights because they're so scared of what could happen to me if they do. I know it's because they love me, but it would be nice to be able to leave the house again and not need Liam to be with me.

I do love his company, though, so it's just another excuse to hang out with him if I need to go somewhere. Most of our outings only include going to the park or to the corner store for slushies, but I always have to be home within half an hour, so it isn't always the most fun.

Sometimes, when it's quiet like this, I wonder about how I've come to be here. I think about all the events that had to take place in order for me to be lying out here right now. I suppose everything happens for a reason. I just wish I could see into the future to know what the reasons were behind me being tormented by Dylan and living through it.

I think about Liam and how much it kills me that he doesn't know how I feel about him. I think of how he'll never feel the same way about me. I wonder how long I'll be able to keep this secret from him.

During sleepless nights at the orphanage, I would lie in bed and think about my birth parents. I thought I wanted to know where they were and what they were doing. Did they have other kids? Did I have siblings I'd never meet? Were my parents even together anymore? I wanted to know why they gave me up and whether they ever thought about me.

When I was really little, I used to think that they would come back for me. I thought that if I was good, and if I hoped and prayed hard enough, they would show up and take me away, and I would have a normal life with them. As years passed, I eventually gave up that dream and came to the understanding that they were never coming back. But I'd become bitter by then. I hated them for abandoning me, and I no longer wanted to know who they were. It took a long time until I finally stopped hating them and forgave them. It still makes me sad sometimes, but I couldn't live with that hatred in my heart. As soon as I let go of the thought of them, I was able to refocus my attention to things that really mattered, like art. I still thought about them, just not as often. I got used to the life I had and stopped thinking about the other.

Suddenly, the back door opens. Liam steps out and sits down close to me as I sit up. "Couldn't sleep?" he asks.

"No. Did I wake you up?"

"Yeah, but I'm a light sleeper. Anything wakes me up."

"Not in class," I joke.

He laughs. "Yeah, that's true." We stare out into the darkness until he asks, "So what are you doing out here?"

I think about it for a second and then say, "I wanted to feel alive."

"Alive?"

"Yeah. Like standing in the pouring rain. Or riding your bike down a tall dirt hill at full speed. Or feeling like the only person awake in the whole world at three in the morning."

"I know what you mean." It doesn't matter whether he

does or not. He's here with me, and that's all I want. "When my parents used to fight," he starts to say, "I ran. I just started running as fast as I could, trying to get away from all the screaming." He becomes quiet for a beat and then adds, "I thought they would make up, like they always used to, but then they actually got divorced. Running became my safe place. I thought it was the end of the world. I didn't know what to do."

"You never told me that."

"I guess I never wanted to talk about it, 'til now."

"Are you happy?"

"I don't know. I am right now." My heart explodes as he looks at me with those eyes. He continues, "I think a part of me won't be happy until my mom is, you know?"

"Yeah."

His hand is just inches away from me. It's so close. I could just take it.

"This whole thing with Dylan," he says. "It won't last forever. Someday you won't have to see him every day."

"Yeah, and someday I won't weigh only a hundred pounds."

We laugh, and he elbows me in the ribs. "Yeah, that too," he says.

I want so badly to kiss him.

We're quiet for a while, looking around the yard, and then I say, "Next week I start going to the new school."

"That's really soon," he says softly. "Will you come back for just one more day? It won't be the same without you after. I promise I won't leave your side for even a second. I won't let him get to you again."

The birds rustle in the tree again. The sky isn't so dark anymore, and there's a hint of sun peeking out from behind the neighbourhood. I know he means what he says. But I also know that even his best intentions have cracks in them. It's really up to my parents now whether I go back there for one final day anyways. "Maybe," I say.

He nods. "Are you almost done feeling alive?"

"Yeah, I'm done. Let's go."

When we're in bed again, I look over at him. He's already looking at me. I try to memorize what his eyes look like in the dark. "'Night," he says.

"'Night."

Fifteen

"You really want to go back just for one day?" Mom asks, unbelieving that I actually want to put myself in danger again. "Don't you just want to wait until Wednesday?"

She's sitting at the kitchen table reading the newspaper and drinking coffee as the morning sunshine leaks into the house through the blinds.

I've decided to try my luck again. I know I'm going to the new school in three days, but I just want that one last day to spend with Liam, even if it means being around Dylan too.

I know it sounds crazy and stupid, but I can't help it. I know that, come Wednesday, I'll never sit beside Liam again and listen to his pencil scratch against his paper. I'll never have the bottom locker under his top locker again. I'll never go to and from school laughing and talking with him. It will never be the same ever again, so I just need one day.

Just one.

"Mom it's been a whole week! I'm bored at home! I just want this one last day." I put my elbows on the table and look at her desperately. "Please. The doctor said I only had to be away for one week."

"You do realize that you're starting a new school this week, right?" She says this as if I haven't thought about it every day since we went there.

"Yes! I know! But that school sucks, Mom." I let her in on this secret she and Dad aren't aware of. "It's one day!"

"I don't know," she says after taking a sip of coffee.

"Mom, please. All the other kids are doing it."

This makes her smile, but she tries to cover it up after a second to look tough. She folds the newspaper twice, puts it on the table, and then takes another sip. "I don't know. I don't like the idea of you being there."

"Mom, please. You're already making me go to a school that I don't want to go to. Let me have six hours longer to spend with him. Please?"

She thinks about it slowly and finally says, but not without complete and total lack of enthusiasm, "Fine. I guess so. But remember, I'm doing this for you."

"Thank you!" I say, throwing my head back dramatically.

"But if one more thing happens tomorrow—"

"It won't! I promise!"

She sighs. "How's your bruise?"

I pull up my shirt. "It's almost gone. I'll be fine." She gets a quick look at it before I pull my shirt back down. "Don't worry," I reassure her.

"That's the thing you don't understand," she says as she rests her head in her hand on the table. "I'll always worry about you."

I give her a quick kiss on the cheek, ignoring her sweet and scared words. "I'm gonna go see Liam! I'll be back later. Thank you, Mom!" I say as I run for the front door.

I ride the one-minute bike ride over to his house, drop my bike at the gate, and ring the doorbell. I'm so full of energy, but I'm out of breath when Liam answers the door. "Liam!" I gasp for air, "my mom said I can go to back to school for Monday." I never thought I'd be excited to hear myself say that.

"That's awesome!" he says. He looks at my bike crashed by his gate. "I'll get my bike and meet you around."

We ride our bikes as far as we can in and out of neighbourhoods and parks, and then we ditch them in a pile and run up the tallest hill we can find. We're out of breath, and I haven't felt so good in such a long time. We fall onto the grass and lie there for what seems like forever. I close my eyes while the world spins around me.

"I'm gonna miss you," he says beside me.

I can't even begin to explain how much I'm going to miss him.

"Me too," I say.

*   *   *

My very last day at school is long and boring. I'm in the second last class of the day waiting for it to be over. I've already said goodbye to most of my teachers and handed in the last of my homework. Although, I'm not sure that it matters much for my grades any more. Dylan's here, but he's staying away, and I'm grateful. I'm sitting beside Liam in class, staring out into nothing, when the bell rings and everyone bolts to the door. "Remember your assignments are due on Wednesday!" Miss Fern shouts over the commotion.

Dylan walks past me on his way to the door, and I freeze up as his eyes dig shallow graves in my soul. "Why are you still here?" he asks.

I watch him leave and think that after today I'll never have to see him again. So I'm okay. I'm about to get up when I feel Liam's hand on my back and decide to stay seated.

"Just ignore him," he says.

I don't say a word. I'm too busy concentrating on how much I like the way his hand feels. It isn't too light or too heavy. Unexpectedly, I feel him move it down my back. I quickly grab my bag and get up, unsure of what to do about it and he immediately pulls his hand away.

"We'd better get to last class," I say.

"Yeah."

After school, we walk home together for the last time. Trees around the neighbourhood have started blossoming. Soon everything will be new again. Up ahead, a black-and-white cat dashes out of a bush, running for its life across the empty street. An orange cat chases after it.

I can't explain how much weight is lifted off me knowing that after today I'll never have to see Dylan again. I just pray there isn't a Dylan waiting for me at the new school. *But what are the chances?*

Liam's been quiet the whole walk home. Eventually he says, "I can't believe this is the last time we'll do this." I nod. I'm afraid that if I speak I'll break into tears. "We'll still see each other though, right?" he asks.

"You couldn't *keep* me away from you," I manage to say while holding myself together.

I'm glad he smiles.

"Don't forget to call me after school on Wednesday," he says when we reach his house. "I want to hear about everything."

"I will."

I desperately want to hug him, but I don't. Instead, I watch as he smiles and walks up to his house. I walk home.

When I walk through the front door, I find that a box has come for me in the mail. Mom smiles disturbingly at me as she hands it over.

I stand in front of the bathroom mirror staring at my new school uniform. Navy pants, starched white shirt, and a tie. To say it looks like the worst thing I've ever tried on would be an understatement. I can't wait to tear it off and put on a T-shirt. "I look stupid," I say to Mom as she leans against the doorframe of the bathroom.

"It looks great, hun," she assures me. However, there's a small grin climbing its way back onto her face. I didn't know she'd brought her camera, and before I can stop her, she snaps a picture of me. "I'm sending it to your grandparents!" she threatens as she runs down the hall.

"Mom! No!" I plead, chasing after her down the stairs.

"Just wait 'til your dad gets home and sees this!" she laughs.

*   *   *

My first day at West Pointe could not have been stranger. It wasn't awful. It also wasn't great. It was just ... fine. Boring. And ultimately weird, compared to my old school. Take, for instance, the uniforms that we're forced to wear. The awful long-sleeve dress shirts and itchy navy pants. Oh yeah, and the tie. I hate that tie. The strange thing about that is, though, that no one else seemed to mind wearing it. The principal informed me that if we have our shirt untucked or our tie is loose we'll be asked to fix it. But I never saw one student with either of those errors. In fact, everyone I saw, from the time we got to school to the minute the last bell rang, looked perfectly pristine and even happy to wear them.

Another thing that made me feel out of my comfort zone was the fact that everyone acted and talked as if they were mature beyond their years—as if they were all adults. There were the occasional runners and screamers in the hall, but it was mostly kids late for class or packs of girls huddled tight at one locker squealing over a magazine. I never witnessed anyone thrown against their locker or kicked in the hall, but I guess that was the whole point of going there. Nevertheless, I still flinched when a locker door beside me was closed suddenly.

Liam and I are sitting on his bedroom floor amongst piles of homework while I tell him the tales of my day. I'm back in my regular, familiar clothes. He watches me intently, but I sense that there's something he's keeping from me. "Is everything okay?" I ask him.

"Yeah. Tell me more about your day," he insists.

I don't want to push the issue, so I begin to tell him about how no food fights were started in the cafeteria at lunch. He laughs and says he wishes he could have seen civilized humans for a change.

A car door slams shut outside. I follow Liam, who gets up quickly to see who it is. At the window, we watch as a man walks up to the house. He's carrying a bouquet of yellow flowers. We listen as he rings the doorbell downstairs. "Is that the same guy?" I ask.

Liam nods beside me. "He was here every night last week. I can't stand him," he says.

It's Mrs. Eriksson's new boyfriend. They've been seeing each other for six weeks. Four weeks too long, according to Liam two weeks ago.

We listen as Liam's mom answers the door and lets him in. "You should probably go," he says. "He doesn't like it when I have friends over on school nights."

"But it's your house," I tell him. "Shouldn't that be up to you and your mom?"

"You would think so," he sighs and moves his eyes to the floor. "I wish she'd just break up with him."

We clean up our stuff and Liam says goodbye to me at the door. I wave once more from the sidewalk before he closes the door, and then walk home.

At dinner tonight, I play with my food and roll my eyes while my parents talk to themselves. Mom's showing Dad the pictures she took of me on Monday. He'd seen them that night but requested another viewing. I don't know why. They're awful and should be burned. He laughs so hard at them. After a while, I start to daze out.

I was sitting on a swing on the playground by my house. Twisting it up tight and then letting it spin 'til I was dizzy. The playground was empty except for a couple of kids and their parents. The evening air was warm, but I still felt cold inside. Through the spinning, I saw a figure walking up to me. I dug my shoes into the sand when the swing untangled. Liam stood in front of me.

"Hey," he said.

"Hey."

He sat on the second swing and twisted to face me, but I found my shoes very interesting. "I heard what happened," he eventually said. "Dylan pretty much told everyone."

I nodded.

"I just want you to know that I like you just the same. Nothing's changed between us."

I looked at him, a little surprised and really relieved to hear him say that. Then I exhaled the air I'd been keeping inside. "Thanks, Liam."

He twisted in his seat a little, looking at the sand beneath him. Then I noticed him looking at me. "So ... do you feel any different?" he asked.

"A little cheated," I said.

Just like everyone else, I wanted to be able to come out on my own terms.

My own time.

It didn't work out the way I wanted it to, but I was just glad that I still had him.

"Parker?" I hear Dad say.

I look up at my parents to see that they have worry painted all over their faces.

"You haven't touched your food. Are you feeling okay?" Mom asks.

"Oh. Yeah. I think I'm just gonna take a walk. I need some air," I say.

They look at each other nervously and then back at me. "Okay. Don't be too long, though," Mom says.

I can feel them staring at me as I walk out of the room.

When I'm down the street, I walk towards the playground in the park and see Liam sitting on a swing. I wonder what the chances are of him being there. He looks over at me for a second and then down at his shoes. I sit beside him. We're quiet for a long time.

"I had to get out of the house," he finally says. "My mom's new boyfriend is still over. He wants nothing to do with me. I don't know how she doesn't see it."

I look over at him. He's staring through me with those piercing blue eyes behind his dark hair. A couple months ago, he shaved the sides of his head and let the rest of his hair fall to the right side, to look like the lead singer of his favourite band because—well, because they're his favourite, and he thinks it's funny that they have the same first name. He thinks it makes him look dangerous, but his freckles give him away. It looks good on him. I have to control the urge to run my fingers through it, and I try to comfort him instead.

"She'll see it soon enough," I tell him. "Then she'll move on. You know she will."

He focuses on the ground. "Yeah, you're probably right." After a few seconds, he looks back up at me. "So why are you here?" he asks.

I twist in my swing. "Same as you. I couldn't be there."

"Things *are* gonna be okay, Parker, I promise. You have a chance to start over. Everything's going to be okay now."

We look at each other for a while, and I try to count all the times people have said that to me before. I can't. I study his strong bone structure and his lips before starting to count sand.

"I'm glad I found you out here," I say, looking up at him slightly.

"I'm glad I found you, too."

We stay out for a while longer, seeing who can swing higher, and laughing 'til it hurts. It feels good to be carefree for just a little bit. After a while, we jump off into the sand and start walking back.

When we turn into our neighbourhood, we see flashing red-and-blue lights in the distance. We start walking a little faster to see what it is, and when we're finally close enough to truly see what's happening, I can't breathe. My hand clasps against my mouth, and I feel sick. We run to my house and push past some of my neighbours, but we're stopped by a police officer at my front lawn, which has yellow police tape surrounding it. "Whoa, you can't come in here, boys," he says as he holds his hand out to stop us.

"But this is my house. My parents are in there. I need to see my parents!"

"I'm sorry guys, but you'll have to wait until we're done cleaning up."

I'm gonna be sick.

"Cleaning up *what*?"

Just then, the ambulance parked in my driveway starts up and drives away. I feel dizzy. Through the open front door, I see Dad pacing back and forth, with his head down, rubbing the back of his neck. He's stressed out. I don't see Mom with him, and I feel sick to my stomach. I need to know what happened. A call on his walkie-talkie distracts the cop, and I slip under the tape and run across the lawn. Dad walks out of the house, and I run into his arms.

"Dad!" I cry out. He holds me tight as I look around, half expecting her to walk out too, but knowing she is probably in that ambulance. "Dad, what happened? Where's Mom?"

He pulls away and holds me at arm's length. His face is full of pain. I think he might cry, which makes me want to cry, but instead he looks me straight in the eyes and takes a deep breath. "There was an accident," he says. I feel myself stop breathing. "She slipped in the kitchen and hit her head on the counter." He looks distant as he takes in a deep breath. "The ambulance is taking her to the hospital. I'm going to meet her there."

I wipe away some of the tears that have fallen down my face, and I start to breathe again. *How long had I been outside?*

"Can I go with you?" I ask him.

He looks at me as if I'm broken. "Not tonight, Park," he says. "I don't think that's a good idea. I've called Liam's mom, and she's agreed to have you stay over there tonight."

"I should have been here. I shouldn't have left!" I start freaking out.

He tightens his grip on me, and I can tell he's scared. But he's trying to be strong for me. "There's nothing you could have done. Accidents happen. They just happen. You can't prevent them. I need you to be strong now, Parker. Mom needs you to be strong. Can you do that?"

I wipe more tears away. I know that speech is supposed to make me feel better, but it doesn't. But I nod, because I know that's what he needs me to do. "Yeah, I think so."

"Okay." He motions for Liam to come over. "Now, I need you to go up to your room and pack your things. I'll walk you over to Liam's."

I nod at him, and then Liam and I walk inside, leaving my broken heart lying on the grass.

I grab my bag off my bedroom floor and empty out all the stuff. Some notebooks, pencils, and my sketchbook fall onto my bed, and then I throw some clothes into it from my dresser.

From behind me, I hear Liam say, "Is this me?"

When I turn around, he's holding up my sketchbook. One of my drawings of him is staring back at me, and I don't know what to do. I'm so scared and embarrassed that he found it. My face burns red, and I look down at my shoes. "Yeah," I say.

"It's really good, Parker."

I ignore him, still not knowing what to do, and go back to packing stuff. Stuff I don't even need. Just anything to not have to face what has just happened.

Unexpectedly, he walks over and wraps his arms around me. It takes all the air out of me, and my head soon finds its home against his collarbone. I close my eyes, drop my bag on the floor, and hug him back as I break down and cry. He smells so good I don't want to let go, but the bedroom door opens, startling us both, and we quickly break apart.

I wipe tears off my face and look at Dad in the doorway. "Are you ready to go?" he asks.

I nod and grab my bag before walking out.

"Where did everybody go?" I ask as soon as we get outside. The neighbourhood is empty. No one would ever have known that something has happened here. It looks normal again.

"They've gone to the hospital or to other calls. There was nothing left to do here," Dad says.

We walk down the street to Liam's house, and his mom meets us at the door. She touches my shoulder before I turn to give Dad a hug. "Tell Mom I love her, okay?"

"I will, Parker. Don't worry, just get some sleep."

I let go of him and walk into the house with Liam.

When he closes his bedroom door, I throw my bag on the floor, take off my hoodie, and sit on his bed with my head down and my hands in my lap, trying to comprehend what just happened. How have I ended up having to stay at his house? Why does my mother have to spend the night at the hospital? None of it makes sense. And the more I think about it, the more frustrated I get.

"I don't get it. I was only gone for half an hour," I say.

"I know, but everything will be okay," he says as he sits on the bed with me.

"You don't know that." I say it rudely and regret it as soon as it leaves my mouth.

"I know ..." he says, standing. He walks over to his dresser, pulls out some clothes, and walks to the door. "I'm gonna get ready for bed," he says. "You can change in here if you want." I nod as he walks out and closes the door.

I'm in bed facing the window, away from the door, when I hear him come in, turn off the light, and climb into bed next to me.

"It'll be okay," he says softly behind me.

I sniffle and close my eyes tight.

"I'm here," he says.

Sixteen

Dad drives us to the hospital the next morning. I'm looking out the window at all the houses and then all the buildings as we edge into downtown. I'm thinking about Mom and about the day they officially adopted me, the day I walked into my home for the first time.

———

"So, what do you think of your home?" my new dad asked me.

"It's incredible," I said.

"Would you like to see your bedroom?" my new mom asked.

I could only nod my head. I was so excited. I followed her upstairs, with Dad trailing behind. She opened the door, and I walked in. I couldn't believe that it was for me. I walked to the window and looked out at the street below for a while, then turned around and smiled at my parents.

"This is really for me?" I asked them.

"Of course it is," Mom said. "This room has been waiting for you for a long time."

"I don't know what to say." I looked around the room and then back at them. "Thank you."

Mom walked over and hugged me. "Parker, we are the ones who should be thanking you. I can't even explain what you have given us."

She took my hand in hers.

"Would you like to see the rest of your house?" Dad asked.

I wore the biggest smile. "Yes."

We pull into the underground parking lot and I awaken from my daydream. We're actually here.

"Are you sure you want to do this?" Dad asks.

I look over at him and nod. "I'm sure."

I watch people move about in the sick-looking waiting room. How can they expect people to get better if it looks so sad? Pamphlets sit in containers on the table in front of us. They make you consider for a moment if you actually have the condition they're advertising. *Do I have back pain?*

Dad reads National Geographic, but I have a feeling he isn't actually reading. A doctor approaches us, and he puts the magazine down quickly as he stands up.

"Mr. Knight, it's good to see you again," the doctor says as they shake hands.

"How is she doing?" Dad asks.

"She's stable and her heart rate is doing fine, so she's looking good right now," he says optimistically.

Mom is in a coma right now. On the ride over, Dad told me that she would look asleep. I already knew what being in a coma meant, but I just nodded along for his benefit. He said I should talk to her, because she might be able to hear me. And we brought some of her favourite things to make the room smell like home. They say familiar smells can help a person to wake up.

Some people, when they wake up, have amnesia and don't remember the people around them or even themselves.

Like on TV soap operas. I do and don't want to go in that room.

The doctor turns to me and I stand to shake his hand. "And you must be Parker," he says. He sort of talks to me as if I'm younger. Maybe he doesn't believe my actual age. But I don't mind. I sort of feel like a child right now.

"Yes," I say.

"My name is Dr. Stovatski. Would you like to see your mom now?"

"Yes, please."

He leads us down a few halls and opens a door. I walk in cautiously while Dad stays behind to talk to the doctor. I see her lying there in the hospital bed, her eyes closed and her hands tucked in by her sides. She has no makeup on and she has bandages and gauze around her head. And she's beautiful. I walk over, sit on the edge of the bed beside her, and hold her hand. I stare at her face, thinking that maybe if she knew it was me she would wake up.

This must've been what it was like when I was in the hospital after my suicide attempt. My parents would have been hopeful but not certain that I would wake up.

"She's so pretty," I say to Dad after he's walked into the room.

He looks at her for a long time, and I can tell it's killing him to see her like this. I imagine that she will wake up right now, and we will all go home together, and everything will be back to normal. Waiting is the hardest part.

"Why don't you put out some of the stuff we brought?" he says after a while.

I reach into the bag we brought and place a vanilla candle on the bedside table. I'm careful not to bump any of the medical equipment while I do so. I place her favourite soft grey sweater on the blanket at the bottom of the bed and her favourite book next to the candle. "In case she wants to read it when she wakes up," I say.

"She'll love that you thought of it."

"Dad?" I ask.

"Yeah, Park?"

"Could I have just a moment with Mom?"

"Of course." He touches her hand and kisses me on the head before leaving.

I sit in the chair on the opposite side by the wall and put my arms on the bed. "Hi, Mom," I say. "It's me, Parker." This is a lot harder than I thought. "Dad brought me today, and we brought some of your favourite things, too. Dad says you might be able to hear me talking to you." Tears start piling up in my eyes, and my breathing alternates between gasping for air and sobbing. "I'm so sorry, Mom; I should have been there. I love you so much. Please don't leave me. You needed a child and you found me. I needed a mother and I found *you*. I still need you."

Exhausted, I put my head down on the bed and close my eyes.

––––––––––

My bag was packed and waiting against the wall. I was sitting on my bed at the orphanage, drawing, when Miss Sophie entered with a smile after two knocks. "It's time, Parker," she said, walking over to me. "Are you ready?"

I looked up at her. "I think so."

She smiled, "Okay then—let's go, kiddo."

I followed her out.

In the room, there were two long couches. On the closest one sat Mrs. Hudson, the administrator of the orphanage. Mark and Sarah sat on the other. I'd seen them a few times before. Mrs. Hudson craned her neck towards me and motioned for me to sit beside her. "Good afternoon, Parker," she said. "You remember Mark and Sarah."

I looked up at them and smiled.

"Hi, Parker; it's nice to see you again," Mark said.

"Hi," I said in a quiet voice.

"This is your last day here," Mrs. Hudson said. "You'll be leaving with Mark and Sarah this afternoon."

I was trying to imagine leaving and never having to come back. I tried to imagine what it would be like to have a family. I couldn't. It just didn't seem real.

Mrs. Hudson looked at me, "Are your bags packed?"

"Yes," I said.

"Wonderful," she said, standing up and straightening out her grey skirt. "I'll be right back with the rest of the paperwork."

Then she left me in the room with my new parents.

————

After I woke up, we were asked to leave so they could run some more tests on Mom. Everything about hospitals and tests scares me. What if Mom is one of those people who never wake up? Dad tries to tell me not to think like that as he drives us back home, but I can't help it.

When we park in the driveway, I head up to my room, and he walks to Liam's house. He wants to talk to Mrs. Eriksson about what's been happening.

I'm not looking at anything in particular, just thinking about Mom being in that room and hugging my knees close to my chest, when there's a knock on my bedroom door, and Liam walks in. I feel so relieved to see him. I need him so much.

He sits in front of me. "Are you okay?" he asks.

I shake my head and tears fall down my face.

"Do you want to talk about it?"

I shake my head again and stare at the carpet. I can feel him looking at me. "I don't know if she's going to be okay," I start sobbing. "She seemed fine when I was in there, and the doctor said she was okay. But I don't know if she will be. What if she isn't going to be okay?" I change my position to sitting cross-legged and wipe my face with my arm. I'm a mess. I just can't stop crying. I look at him. "What am I going to do, Liam?"

Suddenly he leans in and kisses me. *He's kissing me?* My eyes widen in shock, but I quickly shut them tight and kiss him back.

I'm kissing Liam.

My best friend.

My first kiss.

This is the moment I've dreamt about for so long, but it doesn't seem real.

The butterflies are in flutter mode. They crash into each other inside my stomach and create fireworks only I can see.

Maybe he can see them too.

His lips are soft, just as I knew they would be. He feels warm and tense, like he's serious. I can smell his skin, and he tastes sweet. It feels as if it lasts forever, but then he pulls away, and we stare at each other for what feels like forever again.

The only noise is the sound of my heart beating against my ribcage. Suddenly everything is different between us. Inches from me, his eyes are big and wide. As big and wide as mine. His expression is full of surprise and maybe even a little fright. His taste lingers, and I want to press my tongue against my bottom lip and absorb any extra flavour. But I don't.

"You kissed me," I finally say.

He nods while keeping his eyes locked on mine.

"Why?" Not that it matters at the moment. I want to keep kissing him.

"I don't know. I just wanted to," he says.

"Liam, I'm so confused."

"I'm gay, Parker." He says it as if it's the most obvious thing in the world.

My eyes widen (even further) at the shock of hearing this from my best friend. Then confusion overcomes me again. At first, I think he's kidding, but he looks so sincere. "Since when?" I ask.

He breaks eye contact first and looks down at his hands. "Well, my whole life," he says, "but I was too afraid to say anything. To anyone. Even you. I'm so sorry."

I think about this for a second and then start to get angry. I quickly get off the bed, head towards the window, and turn back to him. "You mean this whole time! This whole time that I've been pushed around and made fun of by Dylan, you were just like me, and you didn't say anything!"

He looks at me with guilt. "Parker, I'm so sorry. I was afraid."

I think about this for a second. "But you're Liam Eriksson. You're not afraid of anything."

"I'm sorry," he says softly.

"You should leave."

He gets up hurriedly and tries to touch my hand, but I pull away and put my hands in my pockets. I see tears in his eyes and I want so badly to pull him close to me and kiss him again, but I'm too angry. This was not how I'd imagined this moment at all. Not that I'd ever thought it would actually happen.

"Please, Parker. You're my best friend. I'm so sorry," he says so desperately to me. Every syllable that comes out of his mouth is perfect in every way. But it hurts me more than I can begin to describe. He takes a deep breath and tries to look me in the eyes, but I'm too focused on the excitement of the corner of my room. "I have no one if I don't have you," he says.

My heart shatters as soon as he says it. I feel the same way. "You should have thought about that before," I say instead. I immediately wish I could take it back when I see how hurt he is. But I just look at the carpet between our shoes. "Please leave, Liam," I say softly.

He drops his head, and I watch him walk out of my room. A deep chill runs through my body as I stand alone and run my hands through my hair, gasping for air through my sobbing. My knees buckle, and I collapse on the floor.

So that was my first kiss.

Well, if we're gonna get technical, the first time I ever kissed a boy was when I was five. I'd been staring at a boy who used to eat paste during art class. I didn't necessarily *like* him, I just knew I was attracted to him and not the girls who ate paste.

When you're a little kid, you don't have the best judgment—at all. At recess, I ran up to him and kissed him on the cheek in the sandbox. Well, it was apparent from the moment he pushed me away that he didn't feel the same. Life was a lot more confusing after that point. I don't think I ever looked at another boy the same way, until Liam. And here I was pushing *him* away. Life just doesn't make sense.

Seventeen

School, hospital, home. School, hospital, home. That's what my life has become. I had two days plus the weekend off school, but now I'm back. I don't see the point. It's not as if I'm paying attention in class at all, anyways. I may as well be at home or at the hospital. Everything is so screwed up right now. Mom is sleeping. Dad's going crazy. Liam's gay? What happened with that, anyways? That was messed up. It's everything I've ever wanted for four years, so why am I not happy? Why am I not making out with him right now? Well, maybe because I'm at school, sitting alone on a bench, staring at a tree. But that is beside the point.

In my head, I keep replaying Liam telling me he's gay. After days of thinking about it, I still don't believe it actually happened. It's like wanting something even though you know the odds aren't in your favour. Now that I have it, I don't know what to do with it.

If Liam had let me in on his secret years before, would it have changed anything? Liam wasn't the reason why I'd cut myself, but it certainly didn't help that I felt completely alone. Would Dylan have bullied him too? I can't imagine Dylan trying to mess with Liam. I can't imagine Liam ever letting him. As much as he doesn't admit it, doesn't notice it, or doesn't care, Liam is popular. He's a friend to everyone, and nobody has a bad thing to say about him. Ever. If anyone ever tried pushing him around, there would be an entire pack of tenth graders ready to fight for him.

I'd be there too, but I'd still be the first one knocked to the ground. I'd do anything for Liam. Which makes being mad at him so much harder. I want to be friends again and talk to him, but the anger running through me is too persuasive at the moment.

When I bite my bottom lip, I can still taste what it felt like to kiss him.

Dad drives us to the hospital right after school. It feels like the billionth time I've sat in this awful waiting room. I'm holding a magazine I'm not actually reading. Dad's in the room with Mom right now, talking to the doctors. I don't think he ever actually hears anything they're saying.

A guy turns the corner and walks into the dreary room. He exhales dramatically as he falls into a chair a few away from me. I look up at him for a split second. He looks familiar, but I don't know where I know him from. He's probably my age, with short, light brown hair and a smile on his face. I find this a strange accessory to carry around a hospital. Especially the ICU. I look back to my magazine and the article about bird migration I'm not actually learning anything from.

He starts tapping his foot on the cold linoleum floor. I decide I can't concentrate on not reading while he's doing this and toss the magazine back on the table with the rest of the outdated reading resources.

"Anything interesting?" he asks.

I shake my head.

"What are you here for?" he continues.

The only other time I talked about why I was here, I was sitting outside Mom's room. An older lady walked by and sat beside me in the only vacant chair. She was there for her grandson who had been in a car accident, and they were waiting for results from some tests. He turned out to be okay and went home. She didn't ask me why I was there, but I told her anyways. For some reason, I felt comfortable telling her, even though she was a stranger.

I don't feel so comfortable telling this guy.

"My mom's in a coma," I finally say.

"That must be rough," he says.

Obviously.

I think the conversation is over until he says, "My grandma's about to die."

I don't really know what to say, so I just say, "That must be hard."

"I didn't really know her."

I nod.

"Do you know your grandparents?" he asks.

"Sort of."

"Sort of?"

"I was adopted," I tell him. "I don't know my birth family."

"That must be hard. Not knowing who you are."

"I know who I am," I say confidently in his direction. I'm not going to let some guy I don't even know decide for me that I don't know who I am.

"So, who are you?" He leans towards me on his armrest, and I detect flirting in his voice. I decide not to answer. I'm finished talking to him, and I want to go home. "Sorry. Too forward?" he asks.

I look over at him for a second and then back down at the floor. I'm not interested in anything he has to say.

"I'm Weston," he says, offering his hand.

I reach across the few chairs and shake it. "I'm Parker."

"It must be difficult," he says.

Why does every conversation in this room have to have some degree of difficulty? I think.

I wait for him to finish, but it doesn't seem he's going to. "What?" I say, keeping my eyes straight ahead.

"The possibility of losing another mom."

With a disgusted look pasted on my face, I slowly begin

turning in his direction. I cannot believe he just said that. *How can you say something like that?*

I'm just about to move to a farther chair when Dad shows up at the entrance. "You ready to go, Park?" he asks. I bolt to the door before he's even finished his sentence.

*   *   *

One day at school, Liam and I came up with a solution to note passing in class. If the words were unreadable, the teachers wouldn't be able to figure out what we were writing and, therefore, couldn't read it out to the whole class—which has happened on multiple occasions to other kids, and it's always humiliating.

So we would jumble up each word like those games where you have to unscramble the letters to figure out what the word is. It worked. It was brilliant.

Dad was just up here in my room after the doorbell rang. He'd found a folded piece of paper on the front steps with my name written on it and came upstairs to give it to me.

I'm holding it now, afraid of what it says. I admire the letters of my name in his handwriting—a little messy, but still legible—before carefully opening it.

"M'I ROSYR," it says.

Which means, "I'm sorry."

I know he's sorry. But it doesn't make it any easier to forget. I take a pushpin and stick it to the corkboard on my wall anyways. Next to the ticket stub.

*   *   *

It's almost been a week since the accident. Dad spends most of his time at the hospital lately, and he's been a wreck the whole time. When he *is* home, I hear him walking around at all hours of the night while I'm lying in bed. When *I'm* not at the hospital or at school, I'm here in bed, listening to music.

It's amazing how music can make you feel things. Sometimes it's even therapy in itself.

I can't sleep tonight. I've been staring at the ceiling for hours. How did my world fall apart so quickly? I need to have my mom back. It's killing me not having her around to talk to and just be here.

I hear my parents' door open and footsteps walk down the stairs. Then cupboards shut and water runs. He hasn't been sleeping all week. I stay in bed for a while, until I hear the kettle whistle, and then get out of bed.

I find him sitting at the breakfast table and looking outside with his hand around Mom's favourite mug. "Hey, Dad," I say, creeping into the room.

"Hey, Park. Couldn't sleep?"

"No."

"Me too. Do you want some coffee?"

I make a cup and sit beside him at the table.

"You usually don't come down when you can't sleep," he says. "You always end up painting something until you fall asleep again."

"Yeah, but I heard you down here, and I know that when you can't sleep, you warm up milk to make you tired. But when I hear the kettle, I know you're not going back to sleep."

He looks baffled. "How do you know that?"

"I don't know. I guess just from years of knowing you." He puts his arm around me, pulls me close, and rests his head on mine. I could never ask for a better dad than him. He means everything to me. "And I thought you might want someone to talk to," I add.

"You," he says, "are the best company."

We don't talk about her, but Mom is on both of our minds. Instead, we watch last night's episode of Conan.

When the show is finished, we sit outside. It's a little chilly, but it feels nice as we sit in silence. After a few minutes of watching the birds, he breaks the quiet. "So, how are you taking all this?" he asks.

"I don't know," I say. "I'm okay, I guess."

"You know, you don't have to be strong, Parker. That's my job."

I take a deep breath and consider this. "I miss Mom," I tell him.

He puts his arm around me and I rest my head on his chest, listening to his heartbeat. "I know. I do, too."

"It just isn't the same without her."

He squeezes me tighter and I close my eyes.

Three hours later, and I'm back at school. As I'm rounding the corner to head into my English class, I hear a familiar voice trailing out. I poke my head around to see inside, and I'm shocked at what I see. Weston from the hospital is sitting at the back of the class, talking loudly to his friends. I quickly back away and hide out of sight. *What is he doing here?* I think.

Maybe it wasn't him. Could it possibly just be someone else who looks like him? I peer around again. A few students slip into class and block my view, but when they sit down I can clearly see that it's Weston.

Well, this is just great. As if I didn't already have enough awkwardness in my life, now I have to deal with him not just at the hospital but at school too? My teacher comes up behind me and puts his hand on my back, ushering me to join the rest of the class inside. I'd really rather not. He senses the reluctance in my tense muscles and whispers to me, "Don't worry; all new kids are nervous at first. It'll get better."

Yeah, right, I think. This guy obviously doesn't know me. But I'm coerced into the room against my will anyways. I manage to slip in and find a seat at the front of the class without Weston noticing. But if I'm at the front and he's sitting at the back, that means he has a direct view of me. What if he's staring at me right now?

Class starts before I can finish my last thought, and I hear everyone simultaneously flip open their notebooks and click their pens. It all sounds extra creepy when it all happens behind me. Unlike classes at my old school, these ones are eerily silent.

No one talks. They don't even whisper to each other. Maybe they're all passing notes. But I don't see that from up at the front, either. No one even coughs. For a moment, I actually begin to miss my old school. But then I remember why I'm here in the first place, and I stop missing it.

"Are you okay?" a soft voice asks beside me. I turn to see a girl leaning across the aisle towards me. She looks at me with concern, as if something tragic has just happened. "Are you okay?" she asks again.

I nod my head, wondering why she thinks something is wrong. I guess it was an acceptable answer, because she smiles and looks back to the front of the room.

I reach down to take a pencil out of my backpack and suddenly realize why she was concerned when a bead of sweat slides and stings me in the eye. I watch another one fall and hit the green tiled floor. I touch a hand to my forehead to find I'm dripping with sweat. What is wrong with me? Why am I so nervous? I hastily dry myself off with the suddenly handy cuff of my stupid white shirt and try to act as if nothing has happened. I look beside me to see if the girl is still watching, but she isn't. Her eyes are glued to the board, which makes me realize that I'd better start writing some notes down too.

At the sound of the bell, I book it out of the same door I came in. Now, I wonder, and you may wonder too, why some classrooms have two doors, one on either side of the same wall. I don't know why this is, but it just so happens to be the case right now. So, as I'm taking off down the hall at full speed, the door at the back of the classroom opens, and Weston walks out with his friends. No one is paying attention, and before we know it, we've all crashed into each other, with textbooks and pencils flying everywhere, hitting the floor, and my face going beet red. That's when Weston finally recognizes me.

"Hey, you're Parker," he says, pointing his index finger in my direction with a surprised look on his face.

"Uh, hi," is all I manage to spit out before kneeling down

and picking up my stuff. Before I can cause more damage, I tell him I have to go and take off down the hall again. I manage to escape him for the rest of the day until Dad picks me up. But as luck would have it, as soon as I get in the car, he tells me we're going to the hospital.

"If you want to," Dad adds.

It would be stupid to avoid the hospital and my mom for fear of seeing Weston again. I need to be there. So I say okay. I'm sure Weston won't have the same idea and be there too.

Well, I'm wrong. Weston *is* at the hospital when we get there. How did he get there before me? After a quick and seemingly serious conversation Dad has with Dr. Stovatski, he walks back over and, unfairly, tells me that I have to wait this one out just before he follows the doctor down the hall. I accept my fate of reading more nature magazines and make my way to the waiting room.

I spot Weston sitting there as I'm about to go in. I decide at the last minute that it's far too awkward after what happened at school, and I don't want to sit through his weird comments a second time, so I turn to leave.

"Wait!" I hear him say behind me. I sigh. As a Canadian, I'm obligated to turn around and politely wait to see what he has to say. "I'm sorry about the other day," he says. "I was way out of line."

I nod, accepting his apology, because it's easier than holding a grudge against someone I don't know. I then sit down a few chairs away from him.

"So, I didn't know that you went to my school," he says.

"I just started," I tell him.

"Why did you run away after class?" he asks.

Oh my gosh. *Run away?* He makes me sound like I'm a little kid. "Sorry, I get nervous," I tell him.

"Yeah, I can tell," he says with a little laugh. "Oh, by the way, I have one of your books. I'll give it to you tomorrow at school."

"Oh, thanks," I say.

"Or you could come over to my house later and pick it up, if you want."

"Tomorrow will be fine," I tell him quickly. I'd rather avoid having to go over to his house.

He starts laughing. "Meeting like this is so random. What are the chances we'd both be at the same hospital and go to the same school?"

"I really don't know."

"What do you think of West Pointe? Is it any different than your last school?" he asks me.

In my head, I quickly run over the differences. Where West Pointe has uniforms, students without behavioural issues, and a cafeteria where the food stays on the plate, my old school is a jungle, with torn jeans and muddy sneakers, bullies, and more food fights per year than there are new students. "It's more or less the same," I say with a shrug.

He nods, and I turn to look at a painting of swans on the opposite wall. "When I was little," he starts almost immediately, catching me off guard, "my grandparents used to take care of my brother and me all the time. When my parents had a falling out with them, we didn't see them anymore. I grew up without them in my life, so I don't really know them. I guess it just makes me sad sometimes to know that she'll die and I'll never really know her. So I guess I was just lashing out the other day."

I can understand where he's coming from so I give him a nod of forgiveness.

"I shouldn't have taken it out on you," he adds.

"It's okay. I guess we all need to unleash anger on somebody sometimes."

"So what's yours?" he asks and then adds, "Sorry if I'm being too forward again."

I think for a moment whether I should share my life with this stranger before I say, "My best friend—"

"Let me guess," he cuts me off. "You like him, but he doesn't like you back."

"No, it's more complicated than that," I say and then think twice about telling him the rest. "I'm sorry, this is too weird. I don't even know you."

"You kind of do," he says. "I shared a personal story about myself. Now you know who I am. Plus we go to the same school."

Fine.

"Well, it turns out I don't know him like I thought I did. I've been in love with him for years and hid it from him, knowing he would never feel the same. But apparently he does."

"So, why are you mad? Shouldn't you two be sharing a milkshake with two straws right about now?" he asks reasonably.

"But he lied to me. And worse than that, I feel like he didn't think he could trust me."

"Could he have?"

"Of course. I know more than anyone does what it's like to have your secret in the hands of someone you can't trust. But I'm his best friend. He can tell me anything and I'll keep it safe."

"So what are you going to do?" he asks me.

"I don't know."

*   *   *

Liam isn't perfect. That sounds obvious. It's just that I think I'm finally realizing it. For all the years I've known him, I've never witnessed him laughing or making fun of anyone when it wasn't coming from a goodhearted place. For example, when one of us was losing at video games or something like that. I can't put an image together of him telling a serious lie. He's certainly never hurt me in any kind of way. Until now. But those things don't make him perfect. Just a good person. Maybe it's a good thing that I'm learning this now. When you place a person under a perfect light, you hold too many expectations over his head. And no one can live up to that. I still love him for what he is. I just wish my heart didn't hurt like it does.

I haven't talked to Liam in seven days. I can't. I'm too angry at him, and I don't have the strength to forgive. Not yet. He calls every day, but I ignore him. I haven't told Dad what happened, either. He asks why I'm not taking his calls or hanging out with him, but I tell him I don't want to talk about it. Other than the notes, we haven't talked about him.

Sometimes, when I'm standing at my window, I see him walk up my driveway, turn around, and go home. How is it possible to love someone and hate them at the same time?

———————

Liam and I walked into class the first day back to school after the summer Dylan told everyone. It was Grade 8. We walked to the row by the windows where Dylan, Avery, and Ethan were sitting.

Dylan laughed to himself as he saw us coming. "You don't sit with us anymore, Parker," he said.

I stared at him, confused. *What have I done?* I thought.

"Did you not hear him?" Ethan said from the desk in front of him. "He said you don't sit here anymore."

"Why?" I finally asked.

"Oh, I think you know why, Parker," Dylan said with a hateful glare.

Liam took my shoulder. "Come on Parker. This is so stupid." We started walking down the row to the back of the classroom, past Dylan.

"Well, I see it didn't take you long to get a boyfriend," he taunted.

Liam looked over to him. "Hey, screw you, Dylan," he said.

I was so preoccupied with just making it to the back of the class that I didn't see when Dylan stuck his foot out into the aisle. Next thing I knew, I was on the floor. Liam confronted him, grabbed him by his shirt collar, and pulled him up to his height. I pulled myself up off the floor and joined the rest of the class in watching them. Dylan was smiling sinisterly at Liam.

"What the hell is wrong with you, Dylan!" Liam yelled at him.

"What's wrong with me? What's wrong with him?" he asked, pointing at me.

In one quick move, Liam punched Dylan in the face. The class gasped in unison as he fell back onto the desk. Dylan's whole face contorted before he put his hand to his nose, which I thought must have broken from the force. There was blood on his fingers and fire in his eye as Liam shook out his fist.

"Liam, it's okay," I managed to say.

He shot me a look. "Stay out of this, Parker. It's not okay."

I wish I hadn't said anything that made him look at me, because when he did, Dylan returned the gesture and punched him in the side of the face and then in the stomach. Liam crumpled to the floor, holding his stomach tightly. I knelt down beside him.

Just then, Mr. Cameron walked into the room, saw the blood, and rushed over. He saw the crumpled Liam and knelt down to check on him. "What is going on here, boys?" he questioned us all.

Dylan was quick to lay the blame. "Liam started it, Mr. Cameron," he said.

He looked up at Dylan's bloody nose. The whole class was still watching carefully. "You two," he said, meaning Dylan and Liam, "head down to the principal's office. Parker, you go with Liam."

"This is so stupid," Dylan said.

Mr. Cameron gave him a stern look before Dylan got up and walked out of the room, holding his hand under his nose to stop the bleeding. The whole class watched him leave. Mr. Cameron helped Liam up, and then we followed Dylan to the office.

From out in the hall, I heard Mr. Cameron say, "Eyes on the board, people."

How can I be so angry at him after everything he's done for me?

*   *   *

I just can't shake the craving I have for bubblegum today. Dad's at the hospital right now, and he won't be back for a couple hours, so he won't even know if I sneak out to the corner store for just a second. He's been so protective lately. I thought I couldn't be more sheltered than I already was. Apparently I was wrong.

On the table by the front door there's an envelope with my name on it. It's one of those big white envelopes that usually contain a magazine. It's addressed to me, so I rip it open.

Last month I requested information on an art school here in the city. This is it. It's one that Mrs. Sharpe told me about when she said I should start thinking about applying to different schools. I should be happy, right? So why don't I feel that happy feeling that is supposed to go along with this type of event? It doesn't seem important right now in comparison to everything else going on around me. And I just don't see the point in trying to force myself to be happy about my future and look on the bright side after everything that's happened lately. I tear it in half and throw it into the trash.

There's a warm Thursday afternoon waiting outside the front door when I leave. There's also another note waiting on the steps in front of the door. I pick it up and open it.

"ELASEP ROIFEGV EM."

"Please forgive me."

I want to. I really want to. But I'm not ready yet.

I check down the block to see if Liam is around. I don't see him, so I put the note in my pocket and start walking.

At the corner where our streets meet, I try to check if Liam is in his front yard, but it's too far to see. I wish there was another way to get to the store. I'd rather not see him today. I start walking down his street, past Mr. Rube's house, and then one, two, three more houses, and I'm past his. He probably isn't home.

"Parker!" I hear him call from behind me.

Never mind, he *is* home.

I keep walking, but before long I hear him running down the sidewalk towards me. "Parker," he says, putting his hand on my shoulder. Everything inside me wants to melt into a puddle on the sidewalk as I reluctantly turn around. "Hey," he says.

"Hi."

"I—"

"I can't, Liam," I say, determined to stand my ground. Whatever little ground it is that I'm standing on. He looks so sad, and I want to hug him, but I'm still too angry.

"I'm so sorry," he says.

"I don't care," I say, turning around.

He walks beside me. "Please, Parker. Just listen to me."

"No."

"But I want to talk to you."

"I *don't* want to talk to you."

"For how long?"

That's a good question. "I don't know," I tell him.

He grabs my arm and tries to stop me. "Parker, please," he begs. With regret, I shove him aside and walk away, but he's persistent and grabs my arm again. "Please, just give me a second."

"Why?"

"I want to know what you're thinking."

"You want to know what I'm thinking?"

"Yeah."

"Maybe I'm thinking about how my best friend could lie to me all these years. I'm thinking about how much I hate being mad at you! That it's so frustrating to still go to bed every night with you on my mind even when I'm mad at you. Because you are everything to me, Liam! And I love—"

I clasp my hands over my mouth when the last word escapes. I almost said it. But I can't. I just can't. He stands there staring at me. I feel all the words lying in a heap between us. That last unfinished sentence. There. Now I know how he feels about me and he knows how I feel about him.

But why did it have to be in this awful situation?

He reaches out to touch my arm, but I turn and run away down the street. Not the most mature thing to do, but I can't see any other way around it right now.

I suddenly don't have a craving for bubblegum anymore. When I turn the corner, I stealthily look at him from the corner of my eye and watch him walk home with his head down, before I do the same.

*   *   *

At noon on Friday, the cafeteria is busy with high school kids eating. I notice again that no one throws food at this school. I think they actually use the forks given to them at this school. Weston's sitting across the table, trying to get me to divulge more information so he can play therapist. Over the last few days, it's become his favourite game to play.

"I could be wrong," he says with a mouthful of macaroni and cheese, "but it sounds like he isn't very honest. If you two were best friends, he should've been able to tell you."

I shake my head. "Liam's not dishonest."

He shrugs his shoulders, "I'm probably wrong, then." He begins to say something else, but then he stops himself.

"What?" I ask.

"Nothing. It's just well, it seems like he used your pain as a way to get what he wanted, which was to kiss you."

"No," I say. "It wasn't like that at all."

"But he kissed you the same day you went to the hospital for the first time, right?" I nod. "Seems kind of unfair to me," he says.

Weston leaves me to think while he mashes up his macaroni with his plastic fork, making one strange mound of orange mush. I stir my own but don't touch it.

He starts talking again after a few bites. "Don't think you have to commit yourself to one person so young. You're only sixteen. There are so many other people you're going to meet in your life. High school love is just a speck of sand on the beach."

If he knew my speck of sand, he wouldn't think that.

"Do you want to hang out tomorrow?" he asks, changing the topic.

"Sure."

Eighteen

Saturday morning we drive to the hospital again. I'm busy concentrating on the houses we pass. I think if I had to, I could walk there blindfolded.

"This was on the steps," Dad says, passing me another note from Liam.

"Thanks," I say softly. I unfold it twice.

"I NATDEW OT ELTL OYU."

"I wanted to tell you."

Did he really want to tell me? Or was he going to make me think he was straight our whole lives?

"Can I go over to someone's house?" I ask Dad, instead of thinking about the answers to my own questions.

"Whose house?"

"Weston. He goes to my school."

"What happened to Liam?"

"I don't know. I'm still not talking to him. Besides, I'm allowed to have more than one friend."

"When are you going to tell me about this?" he asks about the Liam situation.

"I don't know. Can I go?"

"Okay, sure."

We drive for a while longer, and then I hear him sniffling,

172

followed by his sleeve wiping away tears. "What's wrong?" I ask him. "If this is about me and Liam—"

"It's not about that," he says.

"It's gonna be okay, Dad," I reassure him.

"I know, Parker, I know. It's just a very hard time right now. For all of us." I look at the dirty floor of the car, and then I feel his hand on my knee. "I love you, Parker. You know that, right?"

I look over at him. Of course I know that. I've never felt unloved from the moment they found me. "I do. I love you, too," I tell him. Then I ask, "Do you want to talk about it?"

I see him consider the offer. "If I told you, would you tell me what's going on in *your* life?"

"No," I say honestly.

He actually laughs a little. But just as quickly, he becomes serious again. "Your mom and I had a fight the night she fell."

"What were you fighting about?"

"You," he says bluntly. "Your mom wasn't thrilled about you going to West Pointe. She wanted to home-school you. I didn't think that was a great idea, and we ended up arguing over it after you had left. We hadn't finished the argument before she—"

"Dad," I say softly, cutting him off. "You can't blame yourself."

It hurts to see him so sad. But there's really nothing I can do to help it. He continues driving, and we say no more about it.

The hospital room is the same, with some more flowers and cards sitting around looking pretty. Liam's mom has been here again, with the prettiest bouquet. I sit in the same chair, pulled close to the bed, and look down at the floor.

"I wish you could hear me. I wish everything were back to normal already. I want everything to go back to normal." I look at her. "Dad misses you, Mom. I catch him staring at your picture in the living room when I walk into the kitchen. We can't live without you." I take her hand in mine and beg, "Please, Mom. Just wake up. You have to."

Just then, the door opens and Dad walks in. He pulls ten dollars from his pocket and holds it out to me. "You've been in here a while. You must be getting hungry. Why don't you go downstairs and get something from the cafeteria?"

"I'm really not hungry right now," I tell him.

"Okay, well, just take it anyways. You might get hungry later."

I stand up, taking the hint. "Okay. Thanks, Dad."

He tousles my hair before I walk out of the room. In the waiting room, I find a lonely couch, lie down on my stomach, and shut my eyes.

Later in the day, I go with Weston to his house. We leave our bikes on the driveway and walk up the steps. I really can't stress enough, though, that it's more like a mansion than a regular house. Tall front doors lead into an even taller foyer, with a crystal chandelier hanging from the second-storey ceiling. The sound of our footsteps echoes off the marble floor. I've never been in a house like this before. It reminds me of school, which is weird. Nobody else is home, leaving it eerily empty and cold. He tells me he's usually at home by himself, and I feel bad for him.

In his room, I spin until dizzy on his desk chair as he paces the floor. We've been talking about Liam for close to an hour. I've never actually opened up to anyone about my feelings for Liam before. Except for the psychologist. I'm actually kind of relieved to let some stuff off my chest, and Weston seems to be having fun playing therapist again.

"Maybe you don't want to call him because you don't want to talk to him. Maybe you want something else," Weston tells me on a turnaround from his closet.

"There's no way," I assure him. "I've never felt this way about anyone else."

"Well, how do you know if you haven't tried out your options?" He raises an eyebrow as he says this and tilts his head towards me. His lips purse into a tiny, curious grin.

I slow the chair down, stand up slowly, and walk over to the tall window. "What do you mean?"

Suddenly I feel him behind me. He stops me in my tracks, placing one hand flat on my chest and brushing the other one slowly down my arm. He presses his body up against mine, and I feel him breathe against my neck as he tilts his head down. Everything catches me off guard, and I try to think of what I'm supposed to do in this situation, but I can't think of a single thing. My brain is completely failing me right now. *I've seen this in movies,* is the only thought that passes quickly through my head. Of course, in those movies it's always some love scene where the girl (I guess that's me, in this circumstance) closes her eyes and falls into the guy's embrace. And obviously, this is nothing like that.

Maybe he's just kidding. You know, just playing around or whatever. I'm sure he'll pull away and start laughing, tell me he was just joking. And then I'll laugh too and forget about it. Hopefully.

Weston's touch is sensual and careful, though. Once my brain catches up with what's happening to my body, I realize that I've never been touched like this before. Weston then turns me around and pulls me aggressively close to him. So close that our knees collide and our thighs graze each other's. His hands are wrapped too tightly around my upper arms as he leans forward and starts kissing my neck. *This isn't good,* I think. *This is not what I came here for.* I begin squirming to get free.

I notice while his jaw is pressed up against mine that he smells good. But he doesn't smell like Liam. He doesn't awaken the butterflies the way Liam does. In fact, I think he scares them into hiding. And I think to myself that now, more than ever, I need Liam. I wish I hadn't come here.

I continue struggling to get free, but he's a lot stronger than I am and gets his way. "What are you doing?" I finally ask him.

He whispers in my ear, "I want you."

Okay, now I'm past being a little freaked out. This doesn't seem to be a joke to him. I think he's pretty serious about this.

And I'm panicking. I've seen this part in movies too. Well, only the R-rated ones I watch when my parents are out of the house or asleep. And they never end well.

"I don't want you," I tell him, desperately trying to tear myself away from his grasp.

He lets go of my arms, and for a second I think that it's over, until he slaps me hard across the face and forcefully pushes me onto his bed. *What was that for?* I want to ask, but I don't dare at this point. The sensation of tears starts to build up behind my terrified eyes. I don't want him to see, but I look up at him as he stares down at me. I have no idea who this person is. In fact, I *really* have no idea who this person is. I just met him less than a week ago, and now I'm alone with him in his big, empty house, and he's slapping me across the face *and he wants me?* What have I gotten myself into? I really shouldn't be here. I want to get out.

However, the look in his eyes says something different. The determination. Of finishing this.

My entire body begins tensing up. My cheek begins to burn where he hit me. A thousand thoughts ambush my mind. I scramble up to the head of his bed in an attempt to force myself into a ball, but Weston takes hold of my ankles and pulls me back down until I'm lying flat on my back. He forces himself on top and straddles me. The weight of his body pressing down keeps my legs pinned to the bed. He uses his strength to manoeuvre my unwilling arms above my head and holds them there tightly with his hands. He starts kissing my neck and jaw again while he has me pinned down. I try to struggle my way out, but he's just so much bigger than I am, and it's no use.

I feel powerless, helpless.

"Don't worry. You're going to like this," he tells me in a disturbing whisper in my ear. He pushes himself up to look at me, and his eyebrow arches again. He smiles as his eyes narrow and look me up and down. I'll never get that smile out of my head for as long as I live.

I try to think of a way to get out of here as he begins letting one of his hands go from the hostage situation above my head. He quickly repositions and keeps his one hand locked tightly on both of mine. My knuckles clash together as he squeezes my fists tight. If his elbow wasn't bent beside my ear, his arm would be resting right against my face.

I think for a moment that I might have a chance to twist my way out from under just one arm. But his one is still stronger than both of mine put together. With his free hand, he begins to trace me. His index finger slides slowly down my chest to my stomach. It stops at the top of my jeans and he runs it just beneath the fabric from hip to hip.

I imagine quickly that this must be something two willing participants would have fun doing together—but with both sets of hands being free. And without the menacing looks and scared-to-death feeling. And definitely not as rough and violent as this. I've had repressed daydreams of doing this sort of thing with Liam. I am not willing, though. This is not fun. And Liam is not here. And now I can't imagine feeling anything except terror about this act in the future.

The future.

He secures his hand around my left hip and squeezes it. He caresses his thumb over my hipbone. I squirm under the pressure and try to push his hand away, twisting my torso, trying to kick my legs.

"Please don't do this, Weston," I beg him as tears well up in my eyes. "Please."

He ignores me and drags his hand across the front of my jeans. He then runs his hand down inches of my leg and looks up at me with this knowingness in his eyes that scares me beyond belief. I know what he's expecting to happen down there, but it isn't.

I'm struggling, trying desperately to fight him off as I twist under his weight, hoping his arm will give out or he'll grow a heart. But he's insistent on getting his way. I have to stop what he's trying to do before he decides to do it himself.

"Don't worry, it'll be fun," he whispers while attempting to undue the button on my jeans with one hand. "You know you want to."

Okay, that's it! I am not going to let this happen!

I cannot let this happen!

I will not let this happen!

With all my strength and with all the anger rushing through me, I throw my arms up over my head and bring them back to hit him in the chest. His arm flies off mine to grasp his injury, and I'm almost free. As he tends to his wound, clutching his shirt with his fist, I quickly pull one knee up and use it as a shield in case he retaliates, while I prepare to scramble off the bed and get the hell out of here. When he comes back at me, he does so with added force and tries to grab my arms again. So I punch him in the face before he has a chance to, and I bolt out of his room as fast as I can.

I'm halfway down the stairs when I realize three things.

One: That was the first time I ever punched someone.

Two: Next to the accident, that was the scariest moment of my life (almost drowning is third).

Three: I need to call Liam—soon.

My bike is still waiting for me outside by the front steps. I pedal down the driveway and away from this nightmare with more speed than I've ever conjured up before. My laces are untied, and hot tears roll down and sting my cheeks. I'm not even sure if the button on my jeans is done up. I don't care. I'm just determined to get out of here.

I scare Dad when I get home. He's walking to the kitchen, sorting through mail, when I burst through the front door, run over and wrap my arms around him tightly. I feel like a child who just scraped his knee on the road, and all I want is my dad to hold me and make it better.

"Hey, you're home early," he says. When I don't answer, he begins to worry. "Parker?" he asks, alarmed. He turns around in my embrace and holds me back. Then he notices my face, the burning red mark that must look out of place on my pale skin. He gasps a little in horror and touches it lightly. "What happened?"

I begin to cry all over again and bury my face in his chest. He pulls me closer to him and places his hand protectively around my head.

––––––––––

"Tell me more about Liam," the psychologist said.

I was still trying to figure out what was behind the colours in that stupid painting. I'd been there for weeks. Why couldn't I figure it out? I turned to him quickly at the mention of Liam's name, as if I were surprised to hear someone else say it. "Liam?"

"Yes, I'd like to hear more about him."

"Oh, well, Liam's great. He's my best friend."

"How did he react when everyone found out your secret?"

I thought about this for a second. "He's the only one at school who treated me like nothing had happened."

"He sounds like a good friend."

"He is."

––––––––––

Later on, I'm forced to tell Dad what happened, and like I knew he would, he totally freaks out. He's ready to go over to Weston's house and talk to him and his parents, but I plead with him not to. I don't need any more excitement in my life. Especially not tonight. I really just want to go to bed. He's not sure about my choice, but he says he's just glad I'm okay. I don't entirely believe that he won't go over there, though. Or at least talk to our principal. But with no proof, how do you make a case?

I follow him into the kitchen to say good night. He takes two bottles of water out of the fridge and asks me if I want one. "No thanks. I'm just gonna go to bed now," I say.

"Parker, I think we need to talk." I don't like the sound of his voice. He puts one bottle on the counter. "Come sit with me," he says. I follow him into the living room and sit beside him on the couch. "I think you need to tell me what's been going on between you and Liam. You haven't talked to him in over a week. Did you have a fight?"

I can only look at the floor. I don't want to talk about it now.

"Parker, please," he goes on. "You know you can always tell me anything."

"I know."

"Then why can't you tell me what's bothering you? Do you not like him anymore?"

I inhale and look at him, "Liam told me he's gay, Dad." I pause for emphasis. "I asked him why he hadn't said anything earlier, why he would let me take the beatings that Dylan gave to me and not say anything."

"What did he say?"

"He said he was scared."

"Weren't you scared when you first told people?"

Why is he taking his side? "Well ... yeah. But this is different, Dad."

At least I think it is.

"Well, all I know is that you two have been the best of friends since you met. I would hate to see you lose that friendship with him over this."

Over this. He makes it sound like nothing. But it *is* something. "But I'm too angry, Dad."

He sits closer and puts his arm around me, driving me into his chest. "You're a smart kid, Parker," he says. "I know you'll make the right decision in the end."

That means he knows I'll forgive him.

It's a trick parents love to do.

He lets me go and then reaches out to touch my cheek before he kisses me on the side of my head. "Get some sleep now, baby."

I lean into him once more and close my eyes before getting up and walking around the couch. I notice him looking at Mom's picture on the fireplace mantel and stop. "I miss her too," I say. He turns around and gives me a sympathetic smile before I walk upstairs with my head down.

My hoodie is first to be thrown on the floor in my room. The phone sitting on my nightstand stares at me as I leave the room.

In the bathroom, I splash freezing water over my face and lean on the counter, staring at myself in the mirror.

My shoes are second and third to be thrown across the room as the phone continues to stare at me. Eventually I grab it and dial Liam's number.

After a couple rings, he picks up. "Hello? ..."

I listen to his voice, but I can't get words out.

"Parker ..."

I forgot about caller ID. I still can't say anything.

"Parker, I know it's you ..."

I hang up. I can't do it. I'm still so upset. I'm mad about being angry at him, and I'm frustrated that I can't find the words to tell him or to forget about the whole thing. Either way, it makes me angry enough to throw the phone across the room and watch its shell break apart when it hits the wall.

I'm so explosive at this point, and I'm breathing hard. I stand up, grab the pillow closest to me, and throw it onto the floor, screaming. It's followed by the comforter. I rip the case off the other pillow and throw them both across the room. They hit the window.

Within seconds, Dad bursts into the room with a worried look on his face. He sees the destruction I've created and me standing in it. "What happened here?" he asks. "What's wrong?"

"I love him!" I scream it as loudly as I possibly can.

Before I can begin to think again, I'm in his arms with my eyes shut tight. "I know," he repeats soothingly to me.

"You know?"

"Of course. I'm your dad. I know stuff about you."

I'm so relieved that I finally let it out, but I don't understand how he already knows. It doesn't matter, though. I hug him tighter.

"Why am I so angry at him?"

"Because he hurt you. You don't deserve to be hurt, Parker. But Liam does deserve to be forgiven. You owe him that much as his friend. Besides, the fact that he's called every day for the past week must mean something to you."

I nod and yawn. "I'm so tired."

He pulls away and holds me out in front of him. "Of course you are." He looks around the room. "Destruction always tires a person out," he says.

"I'm sorry."

He kisses me on my forehead. "Just try to get some sleep."

He takes the comforter and the pillow that still has its case and tosses them on the bed. Then he gives me a smile and leaves me standing in my room alone. I'm so exhausted. I crawl into bed with my jeans on and fall asleep.

Nineteen

The morning after, I'm sitting on the floor under my window, trying to fix the phone I broke, when there's a knock on my door. Assuming it's Dad again, I tell the door I'm still not hungry.

But instead of Dad, Liam walks in. I look up at him. He looks the same, yet different, somehow. He closes the door and stands by the desk. He doesn't look down at the carpet or around the room. His eyes are entirely fixed on me.

"Hi," he says softly.

"Hi."

"Parker, I'm sorry. I'm so unbelievably sorry. I should have told you. I should have told everyone when they were being mean to you."

I look back at the phone in my hands.

He continues, "These past weeks have been the worst weeks of my life. I don't know who I am without you." He takes a deep breath. "I love you, Parker."

At those words I look up, and suddenly it doesn't matter why I was mad at him. The only boy I know I'll ever love just said he loves me. All my anger seems to fall off me as I stand up, toss the phone aside, and walk over to him. I take the side of his face in my hand and kiss him like I've always wanted to kiss him. He kisses me back and puts his hands on me while the whole world stands still for ten seconds. I feel dizzy. The butterflies multiply in my stomach and crash into each other. My heart bursts into a multitude of colours. Overwhelmed, I pull away for a second to gasp for air.

"I love you too," I tell him, barely able to breathe. I've waited forever to tell him those words.

He smiles. We kiss again. He pulls away. "What happened to your face?" he asks.

I don't explain. I just kiss him again, and he seems to be okay with this arrangement. My knees become weak, and I fall onto them, taking him with me. After a while, we break apart, and I look at this boy I thought I knew. He's different now. We're different now. And I never thought we'd be so similar for each other.

"Nothing will ever be the same again," I tell him.

He smiles. "I hope not."

––––––––––

We sit against the wall under the window with my head on Liam's shoulder. We don't talk. We just sit there taking everything in. I did eventually tell him about what happened to my face, and just like Dad, he was ready to go find Weston and fight him (Dad wouldn't have actually fought him)—even though he doesn't know where he lives or even what he looks like. When Liam raced for my bedroom door, I had to tackle him and hold him down on the ground, which wasn't awful for either of us. A little weird, but in a good way, because I've never been able to just do that before for whatever reason. I think he let me be the stronger one this time when he resisted the urge to free himself from my grasp on him. I can still taste him on my lips as I close my eyes.

––––––––––

"So, tell me about your parents, Parker," the psychologist said.

I looked over at him. "They adopted me when I was eleven. Ever since then I've always considered them my real parents. My biological parents gave me up for adoption when I was born."

"How has that affected you?"

I looked around the room. "I guess ... I don't know." I took a deep breath and let it out. "I guess I felt abandoned for a long time. Growing up, I watched a lot of kids get adopted, but no one ever came for me. I guess I felt ... unwanted."

"Do you think that those feelings have something to do with cutting yourself?"

I moved one hand over my wrist and felt the bandages beneath my hoodie. It would still be a while before they were completely healed.

"I don't know. Maybe."

"What made you stop cutting your wrists, Parker?"

I looked at him.

———

"Are you going to come back to school?" Liam asks, bringing me back to the present day.

"I don't know."

"I miss having you there."

I take my head off his shoulder and look at him. "I want to," I say. "I want to be there with you. But it would be really hard to go back. I don't know if I can face him."

He places his hand on top of mine on the floor. "We can face him together. It's time to end this."

I think about it, and then I nod. "Okay," I say softly.

Liam's right. It is time to end this. It's time to get off the floor and fight back. We've put up with Dylan for far too long. I'm tired of being scared to go to school. I never want to have to skip class because I'm afraid of what he'll do to me. I'm done with crying and bandages and getting special treatment because I'm the victim. I will no longer accept that this is my fate. I *like* who I am. And I won't let somebody push me around because I'm not what they like or think I should be. I've had Liam to fight for me up 'til now, but it's time I finally learn to fight for myself. If I've learned anything from knowing Weston, it's that I'm able to.

It's time to be strong.

It's time to take a stand against bullying.

It's finally time to take a stand against Dylan.

Perhaps I can learn to save myself.

The next morning, Dad informs me that I'm not going back to West Pointe, so I have the day off. I spend it at the hospital reading Mom's favourite book to her.

As soon as we walk into the kitchen this evening, Dad turns to me, and he looks very serious. "You never wanted to go to that new school, did you?" he asks. I shake my head. "You'd rather be with Liam?" I nod, already getting my hopes up. "Okay. I talked to Mr. Morrison at your old school today, and he agreed to let you come back. But you're going to be watched like a hawk by the entire school staff, okay? And next year, and for the rest of high school, you won't have any classes with Dylan. If he lays one more hand on you, he's expelled from that school—as he should've been already."

I'm so excited I can't hold it in. But he isn't smiling yet. "When?" I ask.

"You'll go back in two days. But I have a few conditions first," he says. I nod. *Anything*, I think. He continues, "Whenever you have a problem, you are going to come to your mom and me first, okay?" I nod. "You have to work extra hard to catch up on all the homework you've missed." I nod again. "And you are not allowed to be more than three feet away from Liam at any given time. Okay?"

He has no idea how easy that last one will be. I smile and hug him tight. "Thank you, Dad."

I don't think he smiles. He simply hugs me back tighter.

*   *   *

Sitting beside Mom in the hospital room and holding her hand, I watch her. "I'm going back to my old school tomorrow," I tell her. I look down at the floor and then back at her. "I really wish you would wake up, Mom. I miss you."

I can't possibly explain how much I've missed her over these weeks and how much I've needed her and still need her.

*   *   *

Today is my first day back to my old school. Walking along the sidewalk towards Liam's house, I see him shut his front door and run down his sidewalk. I meet him at the gate, and we stand there for a moment, both of us excited, awkward, and scared, before we start walking.

"I'm so glad your dad let you come back," he says.

"I'm glad the school let me come back without my passport," I say with a laugh.

When Dad called the school to ask if I could come back, he told them everything that had happened over the past few weeks. They decided that it would be best to let me come to class while my passport is being sent back. As for West Pointe, they also got a call. So did Weston's parents, after Dad found out their phone number. For the time being, the principal is simply looking into the situation. I don't think I'll ever have to see Weston again, though, and I'm pretty relieved over that.

As we walk, I pretend to look down at my shoes while I'm looking through the corner of my eyes at Liam's hand beside me. The school bell rings in the distance, and we laugh as we start running.

We're out of breath by the time we get inside our classroom. We quickly find two empty desks as Miss Fern turns around and spots us. "Parker, it's nice to see you again," she says. I smile at her while getting into my seat. "I hope you boys have a good excuse for being late."

Liam flashes that charming smile at her and tells her, "We don't."

She smiles at us and then continues writing on the board. I take a look around the room, spot Dylan in the back corner by the windows glaring at me, and realize then that I always find him staring at me. I turn back around to the board and take a deep breath while telling myself I can handle this.

During break, I'm waiting for Liam to hurry up and grab his stuff from his locker for second period, when I'm pushed into the cold, hard lockers and, once again, feel my head bash against metal. Dylan walks away with Ethan and Avery in tow. Liam, who has missed it, looks over at me. "Dude, are you okay?" he asks.

I don't answer him. I am so tired of this! I drop my bag and march over to Dylan. "What is your problem, Dylan!" I yell at him.

Dylan turns around and shoves me. I stumble back. "Well, look who finally decided to defend himself. Did you get tired of your boyfriend fighting all your battles for you?" he says. Then he adds, "And you, Parker, *you* are my problem." He says this all so calmly it's haunting.

"What did I ever do to you, Dylan!" I'm surprised by how good it feels to finally let go. I feel lighter as it all tumbles off my chest.

He looks at me with anger as he narrows his stare. "You're not normal, Parker," he says. "I think you need to get some serious help. Your kind isn't welcome here."

"No one's normal, Dylan! Everyone's different! That is what makes us all special!" I shove him back.

"You're not special, though, Parker. You're nothing." He shoves me again, and I take a step back from the force.

Liam rushes over and shoves him back with all his strength. It's actually pretty impressive. "Don't touch him, Dylan!" Liam orders him as he steps back and stands with one leg directly in front of me, protecting me, just in case, I think.

Dylan loses his balance and staggers back a few steps as

Ethan and Avery catch his fall. By this time, everyone in the hall has stopped to watch. Dylan looks at Liam with hatred in his eyes. "Why? Cause *you* want to?" he asks with a sinister smile.

Every student within earshot stands still, afraid to move or breathe. Liam stares him down. "Yeah, I do," he says. There's unwavering certainty in his voice.

At that moment, Liam steps to the side, so we're standing beside each other. He takes my hand in his and stands a little bit taller. I look over at him, a little taken aback, and then join him in staring down Dylan.

Dylan looks at the two of us as if he doesn't understand what's happening, while continuing to fume. "Really, Liam? You too?" he laughs and then says, "Do you really think I can't take both of you?"

I hear footsteps come up beside me from a few feet away. "You'll have to take me, too," a voice says.

I look beside me. It's Daniel, from our homeroom, standing firm at my right side. I've never talked to him before, but I can feel his support for us. I wonder quickly if he has his own battle with Dylan.

"And me," I hear another voice say behind us, a girl this time.

"You don't know who you're dealing with," Dylan threatens the four of us.

"We know, Dylan," Liam says and then counters, "but I don't think you know who *you're* dealing with."

Dylan laughs. But it's a nervous laugh now.

Behind me, from down the hall, I hear what sounds like dozens of shoes hitting the floor and running towards us. They stop close to us. Dylan starts to look over our heads. I start to wonder how many kids are standing there.

"Come on, Dylan. Let's go," Avery says. He tries to pull him away by his shirtsleeve, and I think I see fear start to crawl into Dylan's eyes, but I can't be sure. Either way, defeat begins to show in him, and he takes a step back.

"Whatever," he says. "You're both screwed up." After he says it, Dylan turns and walks away with Ethan and Avery.

We stand there for a while after, still holding hands and watching him retreat, and then we look at each other. We've won.

Then we turn around and notice the dozens of kids who fill the hall behind us, cheering and high-fiving each other. We've all won. All it took was one voice to get it started, and the rest followed and stood up for the cause.

While looking at all these people supporting me and supporting Liam, I start to realize that maybe I was never alone. We all go through battles of our own. They're all different, but in one sense they're all the same. *We're* all the same.

Just like Mom said.

So maybe I couldn't save myself all by myself. But why should a person have to? Especially in circumstances like these. If there are others willing to help me, I should let them. But I also have to try. Because that's how we learn what we're capable of. That's how we discover who and what we are.

Standing up for each other lets us know we're not going through life alone.

*   *   *

Dad's been at the hospital all evening, since I got home from school. He said he was only going for a little while and that I couldn't come, but it's been hours. I don't know what kind of secret things happen there that I can't be a part of, but he's been gone for too long. And his phone is off, of course.

Just as I'm about to roll off my bed and call the police to report a missing person, I swear I hear a dog bark downstairs. I try to remember whether I locked the front door. Not that dogs can open doors. But people can. Maybe a person broke in with his dog.

As I'm thinking about this scenario and crawling towards my slightly open door, I'm met face to face with a real, live dog. But this isn't just any dog. This is Snickers. I jump back and sit on the floor as Dad lets him loose on me.

"What do you think?" he asks me.

"What's he doing here?" I ask.

"He's yours."

"Mine?"

"Yours."

"I don't get it."

"You're not very good at accepting gifts."

"I thought you were at the hospital."

"I was. For a little while. Then I went and got your dog."

"My dog?"

"Your dog."

"Are you sure?"

"Why are you so bad at accepting this?"

"I'm sorry; it just surprised me."

"Good. I was hoping it would."

I've been sitting on the floor the whole time with Snickers licking my face. "Thank you," I say, getting up and hugging Dad.

"You're welcome," he says, hugging me back tight. "I know it's been a rough couple of weeks, so I wanted to get you something to relax you a little."

"I love him, Dad! Thank you." He holds me for a second longer before letting me go. I love him. And I love this dog. "I'm gonna go show Liam," I say.

"Okay. Have fun," he says as I take Snickers' leash and lead him out of the room.

We run down the sidewalk and turn the corner onto Liam's street. Snickers is so strong, *he* pulls *me*, even though he doesn't know where he's going. At Liam's house, I ring the doorbell and look down at Snickers' happy face while we wait. The door opens, Liam appears, and I don't wait for him to speak.

"Liam, I got a dog!" I shout out.

"No way!" He's just as excited as I am. He kneels down to pet him as Snickers licks his face. "Is this Snickers?" he asks.

"Yeah, my dad just surprised me with him."

"That's amazing." He scratches him behind the ears, "You're such a cute dog," he tells him.

"Do you wanna go for a walk?" I ask.

I listen as Liam shouts goodbye to his mom through the open door and then grabs his shoes and sits on the steps. "He's such a great dog, Parker," he says while tying up his laces.

"He is."

"You're so lucky," he says, standing up and walking down the sidewalk to his gate. I smile as I watch him walk in front of me. I'm lucky for another reason, too.

We walk through the neighbourhood and talk. Occasionally Snickers will see a squirrel or a piece of trash and run after it, pulling me with him, while Liam laughs the whole time. I love his laugh.

"Maybe Snickers and Patches can have a play date sometime," he says.

Patches is his two-year-old tabby. He got her when his parents got divorced. She really helped him through the divorce, and he loves her to death.

I laugh, "Definitely."

Liam slowly slips his hand around mine. His fingers grazing my fingers send tingles all the way up my arm and into my stomach. He looks at me and smiles. And for the first time in a long time, while walking with my dog and the boy I love, I feel good.

Twenty

The phone rings during dinner tonight. When Dad comes back from answering it, he stands at the table and just stares at me, freaking me out. "That was the hospital," he says. "Your mom's made progress." I drop my fork and stare back at him. "Get your jacket. We're going to the hospital."

As usual, I stare out the window on the drive downtown.

"I remember the very first time I saw your mom," Dad says. I look over at him. He's looking dreamily out the windscreen, and I'm hoping he isn't daydreaming too hard. "I was walking down the hall towards my next class when I saw her stop and talk to one of her friends. I started walking a little slower as I passed by her. She was gorgeous." He looks over at me and repeats, "Gorgeous." I smile at him. "She was wearing this purple tank top and jeans. Her hair had these natural loose curls in it. She didn't look like all the other girls who were trying too hard. She just looked natural. I couldn't take my eyes off her." He starts laughing. "I pretended to get a drink from the fountain, just so I could watch her a little longer." I've heard this story a million times, and I love it every single time. I think I love that he loves telling it so much. "Then the bell rang and she walked away."

"And then, after a thousand tries, you finally got a shot with her, right, Dad?" I ask.

"Right." He looks over and winks. After a couple seconds roll by and I've gone back to looking out the window, he says, "So ... do you wanna tell me about the first time you saw Liam?"

I'm surprised that he asked me that, and it makes me blush, but I smile at him while shaking my head. "Not really."

He smiles back. "Maybe another time, then." We continue to drive in silence for another while until he breaks the moment. "You know, Parker, that your mom isn't fully awake yet, right?"

"I know, Dad." I hear him exhale a sigh of relief. "What progress has Mom made?" I ask.

"Well, the doctor said she moved her fingers and her eyes twitched. I know it may not seem like much, but the doctors are hopeful."

"I am too."

He smiles.

At the hospital, Dr. Stovatski leads us through the familiar hallway. He stays out there with Dad while I walk over to her bed and try to count all the times I've done this routine before, but I can't. There are just too many.

"Mom? It's me, Parker." Just then, her finger moves. My eyes widen in excitement and disbelief, and I turn towards the door. "Dad!" I yell out into the hall.

They both come rushing in. "What's wrong?" Dad asks.

I look back at her. "She moved her finger."

"That's great, Parker."

"She did it when I said my name."

"She must hear you talking to her when you're here," Dr. Stovatski says. He smiles at me and checks something on a monitor. Then he pats my dad on his shoulder and leaves the room.

The next morning, the sky is dark with clouds. Rain pours down throughout the entire city and pounds the sidewalk as I run to Liam's house. I'm soaked in just a T-shirt and jeans as I wait on the steps after ringing the doorbell. I'm safe under the shelter of the roof.

I can't breathe when he comes to the door, but I feel more alive than I ever have. I try to catch my breath.

"Hey," he says. He starts smiling as he notices my wet hair and clothes. He holds his phone up in his hand. "I was about to call you."

I can only get short sentences out. "She moved!" I say and search desperately for more air.

"What?"

"Her hand."

"She moved her hand?"

"Yes."

"Parker, that's great! Why are you here? You should be over there."

I can breathe again. "I wanted " I pause. "I wanted to see you."

He smiles as rain continues to pour down behind me. "Come inside."

He leads me by the hand up the stairs to his bedroom. The house is quiet and warm. His mom is probably out. He looks over his shoulder at me with a look in his eyes that I've never seen before. It says, *I want you alone and all to myself.* It makes my knees weak. Just the thought of Liam Eriksson is enough to make me dizzy.

He shuts the door as soon as we're in his room and spins me around swiftly, passionately. My hair whips rain droplets onto his face, and we laugh a little. He leaves the water there on his forehead and cheeks. He's still watching me with the same look. I'm watching some of the droplets as they begin to slowly slide down to his jawline.

Liam runs his hand through my drenched hair and takes a section of it. He squeezes his fingers and wrings out the water. Rain falls and soaks into the carpet. He laughs. He lets go of my hair and runs his hand down the side of my face and neck. He puts his hand on my chest and slides it down my soaked shirt to my stomach. Everything I'd been thinking has disappeared, and all I can focus on is the way his hand feels on my shaking body.

I run my hands through his soft, dry hair, close my eyes, and kiss him quickly. He must sense how nervous I am, because he smiles and his face lights up to tell me it's okay. With his hands wrapped around the back of my neck and his thumbs resting just below my ears, he takes me and kisses me hard. Not wanting to miss the chance, I put my hands on his hips.

More water drips from my hair to the floor. He outlines my jaw with his thumb and absorbs any extra rain. He moves his hands down my stomach again, but this time he starts rolling up the hem of my shirt. I do the rest, pulling it over my head and tossing it on the floor across the room. I'm exposed now, in front of my best friend. But this is different than all the times at the pool.

The air chills my skin, but I've never felt warmer on the inside. He puts his hands lightly on my hips and they warm up instantly, but for a second I flinch, remembering my nightmare with Weston. He turns his attention to my face. "Hey," he says softly, comfortingly. "It's okay."

I remind myself that I know this to be true. I'm always safe when I'm around Liam. But I guess an experience like that doesn't just disappear when you want it to. I smile to let him know I'm okay. I don't want him to stop touching me.

He pulls me close and begins to lick rain off my face. I know I'll never be able to forget the way his tongue feels against my skin in this perfect moment. I want to do the same to him, but he kisses my lips before I have the chance.

This is our third time kissing, but I'm still surprised and confused at how this all happened. I'm not going to keep questioning it, though. I'm just going to keep doing it. There'll be time for thinking later.

His lips are soft. Shocks go off inside our mouths as our tongues touch. He takes my bottom lip between his teeth and pulls it a bit. I feel it in every nerve, and it makes my knees weak again. Then he lets go, and we stare at each other. He brushes his fingers down my arm and takes my hand in his. I could have combusted from the sparks. I can barely breathe.

He grins. "How many more sleepovers do you think we can get away with?"

"They don't have to know for a while," I say with a laugh.

"This is crazy." He laughs too, shaking his head in bewilderment.

"I know," I say, breathing heavily now.

———————

We're sitting against his bed holding hands after our make-out session. I'm wearing his favourite grey striped shirt that smells like him. It feels so good to finally be able to hold his hand whenever I want. "I have to ask you something," I say.

"Okay."

"When did you tell your parents?"

He thinks about something for a second and then says, "A few weeks ago." He starts playing with my hand, and I wait for him to finish. "You know, you're lucky," he says. "In the way that you only had to say it once, to both of them. But I had to tell them separately." He pauses again. "I told my mom first, because I was here, anyways. We were having dinner, and I just came out and said it. I'd been thinking about telling her for months, but I was too scared. I wasn't ready for anyone to know. I'd stayed in my room the whole day, walking back and forth, trying to come up with different ways to tell her and having different conversations in my head. I went through every possible scenario I could think of. I was scared she wouldn't say anything or would say something hurtful. I was scared she'd have too much to say. I wanted to say it at the perfect time, but I know now that there just isn't a perfect time, like with you and your grandparents."

I think back to some of the conversations we had at my grandparents', and now some of it makes sense. I just didn't catch on at the time.

He continues, "When I finally felt I was ready, I would walk to my door and turn the handle, but then I'd get scared and walk away. I did that too many times to count. After a while, I was finally able to open the door. But then I shut it a thousand times. When I finally had the door open long enough, I walked out into the hall for a couple of seconds and stood by the stairs. But then I would walk back to my room and start pacing again. I didn't even notice the time, until my mom called me for dinner. I knew that when I went down there she would be able to tell from my face that something was wrong, and I was right. She kept looking at me like I was hiding something. She wanted to know what it was. So, with all the courage I had, I came out and said it."

He looks like he's a million miles away, reliving every moment in slow motion. "What did she say?" I ask.

"She just looked at me for a while and then smiled." His whole face comes to life now. "She said she was a little surprised, but if I was happy, she was happy. I couldn't believe it, Parker. I'd been stressing about it for forever, but she wasn't mad or upset at all. She was fine."

"That's great, Liam! And your dad?"

Suddenly his smile fades. His eyes cloud over with a sad darkness, and he becomes silent for a moment. "I told him one weekend when I stayed at his place. I paced around my room again for hours, trying to work up the courage and thinking of all the ways it could go horribly wrong. I was a little more confident after telling my mom, though, so I wasn't as scared to tell him. We'd always had a really open relationship, so I trusted him to understand." He takes a deep breath and struggles to continue. "At eleven, I eventually walked downstairs and found him watching TV. I was glad his girlfriend wasn't over, so I could tell just him. I stood in the middle of the room and told him I needed to tell him something important."

He takes another deep breath and readies himself.

"He turned off the TV, and I prepared myself. I looked him straight in the eyes, and using all the strength I had to keep from collapsing, I said, 'Dad, I'm gay.'" I feel him shaking and his grip on my hand tightens. I put my other hand on his arm to steady him. "I'd never seen the look in his eyes that I saw that day. He stood up, and I took a step back out of fear. I didn't know I had fear for my dad. He questioned me, but I didn't know what to say, so I just kept my head down and forced myself not to cry in front of him. I didn't want to believe it had gone this bad with him after it had gone so good with my mom. After getting frustrated and yelling at me, he told me to go to my room. I ran away, wondering why I had even tried. I didn't *feel* better. When I got to my room, I climbed out of the window and ran home."

"Liam," I say softly, "I'm so sorry."

There are tears pouring down his face. I can't bear it. I never want him to feel like this. I wipe his tears away, and he looks back down at the floor.

"I'd forgotten my key at my dad's, so after I'd rung the doorbell twenty times, my mom came to the door and found me crying on the steps. She called him once I had calmed down and gone to my room and I heard her fighting with him on the phone for an hour." He looks back up at me, and I think I see the faintest trace of a smirk at the farthest point of his mouth when he says, "I didn't know my mom could swear like that."

I want to laugh at that, because his mom isn't the type to get very angry, but he doesn't laugh, so I don't either. "Have you guys talked since then?" I ask.

"Yeah, he called a couple days later and apologized for the way he acted. He said he should have been more sympathetic and understanding with me. I think those are my mom's words, though. It doesn't matter. At least I finally told them."

"I'm glad you told them," I say.

"Me too," he says as he takes the side of my face and kisses me.

I pull away first and finally ask what I've been thinking for a while. "Out of all the people who know you the best, why did you tell me last?" I'm afraid of his answer, but it's out there now, no going back. And I need to know.

He stares at me for a while and then at the floor as I watch him carefully. When he finally looks back up at me, he says, "Because I was in love with you. And you were my best friend. I couldn't tell you because I didn't know how you felt about me."

"You had no idea that I liked you for years?" I ask.

He shakes his head. "I was too busy looking at you and thinking about you to notice if you were looking at me."

"I was."

"You never talked about anyone you liked, so I just figured there really was no one."

"Well, I couldn't just tell you," I say with a grin. "Up until two weeks ago, I thought you were straight."

"Yeah, I guess," he says, smiling down at the carpet.

I think about all the times I ever looked at him too long and wonder how he didn't figure it out. A part of me felt like maybe he knew but just didn't want to say anything, to save our friendship. I also wonder how I didn't piece together the fact that he wasn't straight all these years. I suppose it'll make sense now when I look back at certain moments, but at the time, it just didn't occur to me.

"I think it worked out okay," I say.

He looks up, "I think so, too."

After a beat, I tell him, "It's okay, you know."

"What is?"

"That you didn't tell everyone before you were ready. I know I was mad before, but you should be able to come out when you want to, not just to stick up for me. You already do that anyways."

"Thanks."

I think I feel braver when I'm with him. I wish I had been as brave as he was when he kissed me. "How long have you liked me?" I ask.

"Since the first time I saw you," he says.

I'm literally shocked. "Really?"

"Yeah." I try to comprehend this. I didn't even like him from the first time I saw him. I mean, I liked him, and I thought he was cute, but it wasn't an instant crush. "The best day of my life," he continues, "was the day Dylan told me you were gay. At that point, I thought I might actually have a shot with you."

So one of the worst days of my life was the best day of his. Good to know.

"What made you kiss me that day?" I ask.

"I was tired of hiding my feelings from you. I didn't want one more night to pass where you went to bed not knowing how I felt about you. Even if you didn't feel the same. Plus you looked so sad. I wanted to do something to make you feel better. Unfortunately, that backfired just a little bit."

"That's true," I say, joking with him, and then I add, "I wish I had been fearless like you and kissed you first."

"That would've been nice," he says sarcastically and gives his crooked smile.

*   *   *

Liam and I are sitting across from each other at a table in the cafeteria when five kids from our homeroom walk over to us. I know all of them, but we've never really talked to each other. They look at us for a beat, and then Todd Philips finally says, "That was really brave of you guys, standing up to Dylan like that." The rest of them nod in unison and don't take their eyes off us. I'm reminded of the day in art class when Todd smiled at me and I didn't smile back.

"Oh ... thanks," I say, looking at them and then over at Liam.

"We've all dreamt of doing that but were always too afraid of what he'd do to us," Casey Jones says.

I had no idea that other kids feared him too. I thought it was just me. It feels strangely comforting to know that I wasn't alone. I don't like knowing that others had to be afraid of him too, but at least it seems to be over.

"We were pretty scared, too," Liam admits.

I look over at him. I hadn't known he was scared. He's always been the brave one that I stood behind. I'm learning a lot about this boy I love.

"Do you guys wanna sit with us?" I ask them.

"Sure," Todd says, and they sit down. The others are Stacey, Anne, and George. And they all seem really nice. Liam and I smile at each other, excited to get to know them.

*   *   *

"I'll race you," Liam says as we get close to the park.

I don't say anything. I just start running to get a head start. He comes up beside me, laughing, and shoves me playfully before bolting past, and I laugh as I catch my balance and try to catch up.

He runs across the sand and jumps onto the tire swing. The park is empty at nine o'clock. He swings back and around with his knees on the tire and his hands grasping the handles. He laughs as he waits for me to join him. I hop on, with my back to him, and I feel him kiss my neck. Every nerve inside me feels it.

I swing my legs around and put my hands on either side of the tire. He sits down, and our knees touch as we both try to catch our breath.

I look around at all the flowers in the gardens and the birds flying from tree to tree, and then I look across at him to find he's smiling at me. I take notice of how the moon casts perfect shadows on his face.

I want to remember this moment forever. I don't want it to ever end.

Liam starts turning the swing, and we keep our eyes locked on each other as the world starts to blur around us. I reach for his left hand in my right, and our fingers entwine. I watch him inhale and then exhale. I want to remember what every bit of him looks and sounds like. When it comes to the final spin, he reaches for my left hand without looking away. When he leans in, I lean in, too, and meet his lips in the middle. He starts spinning the tire slowly, and I laugh while kissing him. I'm losing my balance, but I never want to pull away. I've waited too long to stop now.

Twenty-One

I'm standing in front of the mirror in my room, attempting to tie the tie that hangs around my neck in a mess. I've already tried about thirteen times and finally give up in frustration as Dad knocks on the open door.

"Mind if I try?" he asks.

I look over at him desperately. "Please."

He undoes my efforts and starts from scratch. Nothing he does remotely resembles what I have tried and failed to do. By the end, it's a perfect skinny black tie.

"Thanks," I say.

"Well, I couldn't have you going looking like a mess. How's Liam holding up today?"

I lean against the dresser. "He's still bummed his dad is marrying her."

"I'm sure he'll come around. Some things just take a little getting used to."

"Yeah, I guess." Realizing how late I am, I push myself off the dresser and stand in front of him. "Do I look okay?"

"You look great."

I start walking backwards to the door. "Okay, good. I don't know what time I'll be home tonight. Does it matter?"

"No, it's the weekend. Just have fun and call me if you need anything."

"Thanks, Dad," I say as I head out the door.

"Wait!"

I turn around and find myself in his embrace. He holds me securely and I can sense his fear. He doesn't need to say anything. I understand. I hug him back.

Liam's sitting on his front steps playing with a button on his black vest when I walk to his house. We're coordinated with matching black Chucks. He walks over when he sees me.

"Hey," I say.

"Hey," he says miserably.

We stand there awkwardly for a while. I want to kiss him, but his mom might be watching, and we aren't telling our parents yet. "How are you?" I finally ask instead.

"I'm all right, I guess. I feel better that you're doing this with me." He checks over his shoulder down the road. "My dad should be here soon."

We lean against the fence and he touches my hand. It sends shocks up and down my entire body, making it difficult to breathe. I lace my fingers through his and we hold hands in perfect silence.

It's a really nice wedding, considering who Liam's dad is marrying. Most of the people around me seem very uptight, but who am I to judge them? The wedding is held outside in a garden, and the smell of flowers fills the air as birds sing and call to one another in the trees. By a tall oak tree, a woman plays a harp.

I'm sitting in the third row, beside some people I don't know. The whole garden is filled, and everyone is looking ahead at the bride. I'm dividing my time between watching the actual wedding and staring at Liam, who's standing at the front beside his dad. The whole event seems to move in slow motion. I look over at him for a beat while he's watching the ceremony, and then he looks back at me. Smirks creep across our faces as we stare at each other and try our hardest not to start laughing. I watch him the whole time and think about all the moments I had missed him looking at me and wonder how I could have possibly not seen it. It still doesn't seem real that all of this has happened. I used to think about it all the time, but it's better than anything I ever imagined.

Later in the evening, we're sitting alone at a white table while some people behind us slow dance to the live music, and half-filled glasses of champagne sit in front of us. I'm playing with one of the glasses, tilting it to one side until the liquid almost spills out and then saving it and tilting it the other way. I feel him staring at me, and when I finally look over at him, he looks like he has a plan. He stands up and says, "Do you wanna get out of here?"

I sit the glass upright. I'm intrigued now. "Where are we gonna go?"

"I don't know. Let's just get lost."

"Okay." I'll follow him anywhere.

We make our way through the white tables and he takes my hand in his. His new relatives give us dirty looks, but we don't care. We just smile at them and walk off. Nothing can stop me from feeling this good. When we reach the last couple of tables, we pick up speed and run. There's a garden maze up ahead, and I can tell that's where we're heading.

He lets go of my hand when we're in the maze before turning to look at me and then taking off on his own. I remember that look in his eyes from before, and it makes me excited. I laugh at him and run faster to catch up. Around the corner, I expect to catch him, but he isn't there. A couple more turns around in the dark, and I start walking backwards around another bush.

Suddenly, I'm pulled by my perfect tie and kissed. We laugh excitedly and fall into a bush, making out. The thorns on the leaves cut my hands, as one holds the back of his head and the other grips him securely around his waist. In one swiftly attempted, yet completely awkward motion, he pushes me onto my back on the ground and positions himself perfectly on top of me. Rocks dig into my back, but in the moment, nothing can bother me.

Liam unbuttons the last button on my shirt that's visible before they disappear beneath my black dress pants. As I lift my hips off the ground, he untucks my shirt, revealing the last button, and undoes it. While he's doing this, I tug at his tie and loosen it around his neck. Then I start unbuttoning his shirt at the top. There's a white T underneath. Same as me. I smile.

He runs one hand through my hair, and I run both of mine down his neck, down his chest, down his legs, while we kiss. Then for some reason, he pulls away, sits back against my legs, and looks at me. "Parker?"

I sit up on my elbows. His blue eyes are illuminated in the darkness. They convey a hint of confusion and wonder. His perfect skin glows in the moonlight. I can't wait until he says what he's going to say, so I can kiss him again. "Yeah?"

"Is it weird that this isn't weird?"

I look out into the dark night sky to see the stars lit brightly behind him, and then I look back over and smile. "No."

Reaching out towards him, I pull at his lower lip with my teeth while looking into his eyes. I'm scared, because this is all so new to me. But I'm confident because I know he wants it too. I wonder to myself how I've lived so long without the sweetness of his bottom lip. He closes his eyes for a second as I bite a little harder, and when I let go he kisses me again.

All the hours turned into days turned into months and years that I dreamt about doing this don't even compare to how incredible and astounding it really is. I'm afraid I'm going to wake up in bed one day and this will all have been a dream. I'll go to school and see my best friend, not my boyfriend. We'll do homework and he'll be thinking about math equations while I'm thinking about him. We'll ride our bikes through the park and we won't stop by the ocean and kiss in front of the ducks.

I have to tell myself it is real. I really am holding the boy I love, and he really is kissing me back. Everything is real. So finally real.

We wake up on the ground to the sound of something

ringing. I have my head on his chest. His arm is wrapped around my side, and our legs are tangled together. It keeps ringing as we sit up and look around, disoriented. I crawl on my hands and knees to find the ringing, as he reaches out and touches my leg to pull me back.

I pick up my phone and answer. "Hello?" I stand up, still smiling at him, and fix my hair with my hand. But then my smile begins to fade. "What?" I say to Dad on the other end of the line.

I must look shocked, because Liam gets up and starts staring at me. There's dirt on his knees.

"Okay," I say.

I look down. There's dirt on my knees, too.

"Okay."

I hang up, slowly put the phone back into my pocket, and then look at him.

"What is it?" he asks.

I can't speak. I open my mouth, but no words will form. I look at the ground.

"Parker, what is it?"

"My mom woke up." The words surprise even me.

"Parker, that's amazing!"

"My dad's coming to get me. I have to go. I'm sorry."

"I understand."

I take a deep breath and try to grasp what just happened. We dust ourselves off, and he touches my hand before we run out of the maze.

Dad is parked by the curb, and I start running towards the car while straightening my tie. I turn around quickly and grab the side of Liam's face, kissing him so hard before leaving.

By the time I have my seatbelt on and wave to Liam, I realize that Dad just saw me kiss a boy for the first time. I slide down in my seat and close my eyes, avoiding eye contact with him. We drive in silence for a while, until he says, "Are you excited?"

"I kissed him, okay!" I've never gone red faster. I didn't

mean to say it. It just came out. He laughs at me, though. Probably because he never expected me to say that so dramatically either. I sit up a little bit when I know it isn't going to turn into a big deal. "Yes. I'm excited," I say quietly. I look up at him from the corner of my eye and see him smiling, so I sit up a bit farther.

"I think you two make a cute couple," he says.

"Dad, you don't have to make it weird," I say.

He laughs again, and then I notice him start to eye me closely. I realize that my shirt is still untucked and mostly unbuttoned and my tie is hanging loosely around my neck. "So you had fun?" he asks with a grin on his face.

I roll my eyes. "Oh my gosh."

In the waiting area, there's no one except for us and a familiar woman at the receptionist's desk. When Dad walks over, she looks up and I look around. "We're here to see Sarah," Dad says.

"I'm sorry, Mark, but visiting hours just ended," she says in a nice way.

"But she just woke up," he says.

"I'm sorry. You'll have to come back in the morning."

From down the hall, Dr. Stovatski walks towards us. "Mark, Parker, it's good to see you," he says.

"We need to see Sarah," Dad says again.

"Oh, I'm sorry. You'll have to come back tomorrow."

Dad points down the hall, "But she's right there!"

The doctor nods his head. "Yes, and under the circumstances, I would allow it, but Sarah's sleeping right now. She's exhausted and needs to rest. You are more than welcome to come back in the morning."

I look up at Dad. He looks defeated and tired. "Okay. Thank you," he says before we turn and walk out. He runs his hands through his dark hair and puts his arm around me securely.

In the kitchen the next morning, I'm tapping my foot on the chair while eating the last bites of my cereal. Dad is standing by the patio door, staring intently at something outside—or maybe nothing at all. I drop my spoon into the bowl as I swallow. "I'm finished. Can we go now?" I ask, getting up and walking away.

He doesn't hear me. He's in a daze.

"Dad! Can we go?" I ask a little louder.

When he turns around and sees me signalling towards the door, he just picks up my bowl and brings it to the sink. "Yeah. In a second," he tells me.

I walk over to him as he rinses out the bowl. He leans against the counter and looks out into the side yard. Outside the kitchen window, there used to be three tall shrubs blocking the view between our house and the neighbours'. Last year, Mr. Hodge cut all of them down. We have no idea why. But now our two households can see perfectly into each other's kitchens. It's creepy coming downstairs in the middle of the night for a glass of water and seeing Mr. Hodge just a few feet away in his house. It scares Mom all the time.

"Dad, what's wrong?" I ask him. He doesn't answer me and we stand there silently for a while. "Dad ... Mom's going to remember us," I reassure him. "She has to."

I don't know if it's true, but I need it to be. He looks down at me and then puts his arm around my shoulders. We stay there for another while, staring into the Hodges' empty kitchen.

———————

When Mom wakes up, I'm sitting in the chair beside her bed, trying to do months' worth of social studies homework. School's over in a few weeks. Exams are starting soon and I actually want to do well on them. I've been sitting here for two hours reading about the Canadian government and trying to cram as much information as I possibly can into my brain.

"Parker ..." she says so softly I almost don't even hear her.

I look up to see her looking over at me. "Mom!" I shout. I leap up and hug her. It's been so long since I've hugged her.

She smells the same—like Mom. "You remember me!" I say, suddenly overwhelmed with tears.

"Of course I do, baby." She looks at me just as she always used to. "Please don't cry," she says as more tears start to stream down my face. I smile at her while trying to breathe through the sobs. "I missed you so much," she says.

"I missed you, too."

"How are you, baby?" she asks.

I can barely get the words out. They come out airy and choppy. "I'm so good now."

When Dad walks in moments later, carrying coffee, he sees her and quickly puts the cup on the table. I take a step back as he reaches out to touch her hand. "Sarah ..." Is all he has to say.

"Hi, darling," she says through teary eyes.

"I ..." he says as tears fall down his face.

"I know. Me too."

I turn my head away while they kiss. I'm so glad that they have each other again. Dad calls me over and puts his arm around me as Mom holds my hand. I'm so happy I finally have my whole family again.

"So, tell me everything that's happened," Mom says. There certainly is a lot to tell. I look up to see Dad smiling down at her.

Twenty-Two

The last few weeks, since Mom woke up, passed pretty quickly. Mom is finally coming home today after her long stay at the hospital. The nurses wanted to keep an eye on her, and that was okay with us. I was so relieved when Mom knew who we were. I know that's what Dad was scared of most. I think Dad and I lived at the hospital more than we lived at home over the past couple of months.

Today was the last day of school. All of our exams are finished, and Liam and I both think we did pretty all right on them. Dylan hasn't said a word to Liam or me since that day in the hall. In fact, I haven't seen him talk to anyone else at all except for Ethan and Avery. Oh, and all of our windows remain unbroken. Maybe he has finally learned. One can only hope. We've hung out with our new friends at school every day since then, and we have plans with them for the summer.

Next week, Liam's dad is taking us camping. Liam says his dad wants to try to get to know him again. His mom dumped that guy she was seeing, and she has a new boyfriend now. He's a photographer, and Liam likes him too. Liam says his mom is finally happy.

Mrs. Eriksson and her boyfriend are sitting on the front steps when we stop in front of Liam's yard. He's taking pictures of us, and she's waving, so we smile and wave back. We look at each other for a beat. We're both thinking the same thing.

I can't wait to see you again. But it's more like, *I can't wait to be alone with you again.*

"I'll see you tomorrow," I say after a while.

"Okay. Bye, Parker."

I start walking to my house after turning around to smile at him one more time. He smiles back and then opens his gate and runs up the sidewalk.

"What makes you happy, Parker?" the psychologist asked me one afternoon.

I was still staring at that painting. It'd been six weeks of trying to figure out what it was. It was driving me crazy. How could I not find what was behind all the colour?

I turned to him finally. "Happy?" I repeated.

He nodded.

I thought about this for a second. "My parents make me happy."

"Besides your parents," he said.

I looked around the room and then back at him. "Liam makes me happy."

"Besides Liam."

I studied the walls, and then my eyes were drawn back over to the painting. "Art."

"Ah, so you're an artist, Parker," he said as if he had just cracked the code.

"Well, I want to be," I said.

"I thought you might be."

I stared at him confused. "How did you know?"

He smiled, "Years and years of being able to read people." He probably figured I was still confused, because he went on. "Artists, whether they be painters, musicians, or writers, for example, see the world differently. They feel the world differently. They have a gift of being able to channel the pain they see in the world, and also the wonder that the earth holds, into art. Your life, as any other, Parker, is going to be difficult, but you have this gift to interpret pain and suffering into something beautiful."

"But what if I don't know how to?"

"It's already inside you, Parker. You just need to search for it." And at that moment, I finally understood the painting. I stared at him for a beat, until he looked at his watch and said, "Well, that's our time."

It was a heart.

Under all the colours streaked across it, the painting held a heart. It was outlined so softly and it was barely there. But once I found it, it seemed to stand out boldly.

After that, everything made sense.

In each of our lives, there's a heart. Under all the layers of colours, there's something that we love. Something that keeps us alive. Something we strive for. It's something that helps bring us a brighter day when the last one was dark and seemingly hopeless. The layers simply represent all the things that the world throws at us to challenge how much we truly want what we want. What we're willing to go through in order to get what we're after—things like fear and negativity, or people who push us down when they should be lending their hands to help us get to the heart.

The heart represents something different to everyone. Maybe to some the heart is a feeling, an emotion, a person, an animal, a family, a career, an imagination, a friend, a goal, or a dream. Maybe it's multiple things. Maybe it isn't anything on earth but a dream for something bigger or otherworldly—a heaven of sorts.

For me it's three things. My heart represents finding hope in my parents; a future and a life in art; and love, in Liam.

*   *   *

Tonight Mom and I talked for hours while Snickers lay beside us. I told her all about Liam and about our new friends at school, and she listened intently. She had been surprised to find Snickers at our house when she came home, but she instantly loved him and he loves her back. I never want her to leave again. Life's too strange without her.

She leans over and kisses my forehead. "Good night, darling," she says.

"'Night, Mom." She starts walking over to the door, but there's something I just can't let go of. I've been thinking about it hard for weeks and it's been a lingering thought in my head for years. "Mom?" I finally say.

She turns back around to face me again. "Yeah?"

"How did you know you wanted me?"

She walks back over and sits down. "What do you mean?" she asks.

"Out of all the kids at the orphanage, why did you pick me?"

She looks at me sweetly. "Well," she says, "when we visited the first day, Mrs. Hudson took us on a tour of the building and led us outside where a bunch of kids were playing. She was talking to us about something when I first saw you across the field. You were sitting on a picnic table drawing something in your notebook. I couldn't take my eyes off you. There was something intriguing about you. I knew there had to be something special about that boy, and I needed to find out what it was. When I turned to your dad to point you out, I saw that he was already looking at you too. He turned to me, and we both smiled. We knew individually and together that you were always supposed to be ours."

"I don't remember that," I say.

She kisses me again, and I breathe in the scent of her that I had missed all those weeks. "It doesn't matter," she says. "What matters is that you're ours now, and we love you more than you'll ever know. Good night, darling."

"'Night, Mom."

*   *   *

Liam's waiting outside to go biking this morning. Before running out of my room, I stop at the door, unzip my hoodie, and throw it onto my bed. I don't need it anymore. Liam likes me just the way I am, scars and all. It doesn't matter if they're always going to be there. They're a reminder of how hard life can be and of when I almost gave up, but also of how good it gets if you hold on and just how worth it life is.

The psychologist helped me a lot by showing me how I was destroying my life. After those six weeks, I never cut myself again. But Liam was the one who saved my life. He never let me forget how much I meant to him, and he really helped me just by listening and being a friend when I needed him most. And if he hadn't found me in my room that day, I wouldn't even be here today.

I understand now that when times get hard you just have to stand up taller, face your fears, and not let them take you down. When you let a bully like Dylan scare you, you let him take away a part of your life—maybe even your whole life. But when you stand up against him, you gain that part of your life back. I'm a whole person again, and I'll never let anyone else bring me down because of who I am. I'm not a perfect person. But being gay is perfectly fine with me. It doesn't matter what anyone else thinks.

I know I won't always have Liam to stand beside me and back me up when I face difficult situations, but I also know I've grown and become a stronger person. I've overcome being knocked down, and I stand taller now.

I can stand on my own and be okay.

"Parker?" I hear Dad call from the kitchen as I'm coming down the stairs.

I walk into the kitchen to find both of them standing there. That's when I notice the big white envelope that Dad is holding. "Yeah?" I say hesitantly.

"This came in the mail for you today," he says, holding it out to me.

I take it cautiously and then tear into it. I hardly ever get mail. They're watching me closely and it freaks me out. It's information on that art school. "But I already got this," I say.

"Yeah, but you tore it up," he says. "I found it in the trash, so I ordered you a new one. If you're still interested in the school."

"Yeah, I am. Thanks."

They smile. I hadn't really thought a lot about this since the last package came, but I'm glad I get a second chance at it.

I hug them goodbye and take Snickers' leash before running out of the room. But before I forget, I shout, "The painting's finished, Mom! It's in my room!"

I like to think she smiled and then went up to see it. I finished it the night before she came home, a few days ago, and then did the final touches last night. I was too excited and couldn't sleep, so I took out my brushes and colours and painted 'til three in the morning while listening to the kettle whistle downstairs.

Grabbing my bike from the garage, I meet Liam at the bottom of the driveway. The summer is finally here and I'm excited to spend two months with him before going back to high school.

School hasn't exactly turned into heaven, but it isn't exactly hell anymore, either. I still spend more time daydreaming out the window than paying attention in class, but now I don't fear for my life at every shadow behind me. Dylan and his fists keep their distance—not just from me but from everyone.

Before we race each other down the street, Liam looks over at me with adventure in his eyes. "Hey, Parker," he says.

I look at him and smile. A big grin surfaces on his face, and I know exactly what he's thinking. He can't wait to get as far away as possible from all human contact, ditch our bikes on the grass, and kiss in a field somewhere. I grin back at him. I still can't really picture my future, only bits and pieces of it here and there, but I know he's a part of it, and right now that's all I need to know.

"Hey, Liam."

CPSIA information can be obtained at www.ICGtesting.com
Printed in the USA
LVOW050052161212

311858LV00008B/480/P